THE DUKE AND THE DEADBEAT

Gregory L. Norris

A NineStar Press Publication

Published by NineStar Press
P.O. Box 91792,
Albuquerque, New Mexico, 87199 USA.
www.ninestarpress.com

The Duke and the Deadbeat

Printed in the USA
First Edition
November, 2018

Print ISBN: 978-1-949909-19-7

Also available in eBook, ISBN: 978-1-949909-11-1

Warning: This book contains sexually explicit content, which may only be suitable for mature readers.

Duke Donovan was born into rock royalty. Front man for the popular Goth band 3-D, Duke's had everything handed to him his entire life—fame, fortune, flesh. The problem is he wants none of it. After staging an unforgettable concert performance meant to give him an exit from the spotlight, Duke skyrockets 3-D's rising star past the stratosphere, making the band more popular than ever and Duke ready to crack from all the unwanted attention and pressure.

Seamus Whyler is tall, handsome, and passionate about music. Seamus has had none of Duke's lucky breaks and dreams of a rock star's life while living out of his car between gigs. Meeting Duke is like looking into a mirror—and long last being given a shot at true stardom when the pop prince offers to switch places with the pauper. But as Duke and Seamus soon discover, leaving their real identities behind isn't so easy a thing to accomplish while being dogged by their pasts and a ruthless celebrity music blogger who smells a ringer, and when the opportunity for true love forces them both to face the music.

A-SIDE

Track 1

MAROON 5 STUD Adam Levine had taken to the stage stripped down to his black boxer briefs, black socks, and smoldering Cheshire Cat's smile that insured the other side of his bed would never grow cold. The guys in Blink 182 had turned mediocre talent into megasuccess by conveniently forgetting to put on their pants or underwear before streaking out to their instruments, dicks swinging, hairy butts displayed for the crowd to behold. Before them, Green Day's handsome frontman Billie Joe Armstrong, with his mop of hair bleached blond and dyed neon-green, had strummed his guitar and crooned for the orgasming audience with his lush thatch of pubic curls and limp cock hanging in clear view. After, it was the Scissor Sisters and Queens of the Stone Age letting it all dangle. Once, live on MTV, some hairy Wolverine-looking tool going by the name of Evil Jared Hasselhoff hopped on a crate, whipped out his manhood, and relieved himself on the lead singer of the band Placebo.

Duke Donovan Dalton, the driving force behind the Goth-rock band 3-D, planned to outshine all of them. The Death Heart Tour's final leg, winding through Austin and concluding in Boston, would be the ultimate musical mind-fuck.

"You can do this," Duke said, casting a nervous glance into the mirror.

Harley shot him a look from the other side of the room. Duke's trusted assistant, who also maintained the band's website and social media pages on FaceSpace, MyBook, and Chatter, always knew when something dangerous was brewing, and what Duke sensed now was no different. What would he Chit about, using that economy of a hundred and forty-four words? *Duke looking way too calm. Huge audience, eager to hear the tunes, screaming bloody murder. What if the murder victim's Duke Dalton? I think he's contemplating suicide!*

Harley knew Duke, had since they were kids touring with their dads. An uncomfortable rush of warmth bloomed in his gut, threatening to crack the calmness staring back from the glass.

"What the fuck's going on?" Harley demanded. No one else would dare speak to Duke Dalton that way, not the band's concert promoters, the rock journalists or late-night talking heads. Not even Duke's dad, Jack Dalton, lead singer in the big hair juggernaut, Stage Fright.

"I don't know what you mean," Duke said flatly.

"For starters, you haven't touched the snack bar."

Duke swept a glance across the table. There were plenty of bottles looming over a half dozen bowls, each filled with colorful, tempting vice—big red disks, blue ones, green, two shades of brown, yellow.

Duke marched over to the snack bar, grabbed a handful of green, and crunched down.

"Mmm, peanut butter, my favorite," he said and then popped one of the bottles, washing the candy down with a jolt of lukewarm soda. "There, satisfied?"

Harley watched Duke from the cut of his eye but didn't answer. The dude was onto him. *Oh well*, Duke thought. By the end of the show, the whole world would be. And he was okay with that. Better than okay. Every other day, some new scandal and sex tape broke on the news.

At least he wouldn't bore them.

Shaye Floden, 3-D's keyboard player, grabbed a handful of red candy. He stood in the middle of the backstage clubhouse and dressing rooms clad only in his underwear, a pair of tight-fitting designer whites stuffed to capacity in the front. Shaye had the second biggest cock in the band, inferior size-wise only to Duke himself, and wasn't ashamed to let that fact be known.

"You nervous?" Shaye asked, crunching on candy and scratching at the meat of his balls.

"No," Duke answered.

"Figured you must be, on account of the fact that you look so calm." Shaye flashed a cocky smile and groped the front of his underwear. "Damn, I can't wait to fuck something tonight."

Harley, or the hotties in the makeup team, one of the best in the business... there certainly would be enough holes to plug after the concert. Ladies as well as dudes, depending upon where his tastes went. Shaye's pale blue eyes drifted toward the little blonde thing waiting to paint his face.

"Okay, who's ready to turn into a zombie?" she asked.

"I'm coming to get you, Barbara," Shaye said in a comically sinister voice. He extended his hands. "*And I'm so very horny!*"

The makeup artist—Duke doubted her name was Barbara—giggled and waved him over to one of the chairs. There, Shaye Floden began his transformation into "Bones."

Bass player Arif Yusian, better known to 3-D fans as "Scalpel," entered the room for a drink and a snack. Another makeup artist seized him by the arms.

"Give me five, okay?" Arif said.

"Only if you tell Joe-Kev to hustle his ass in here. We need to start early on him for the full effect."

Joe-Kev Hallet, who went by the handle "Autopsy," soon made an appearance. The oldest member of the band at twenty-seven, his body was a canvas of colorful ink. A sleeve of thorns and roses covered one arm from shoulder to elbow. A tiger slinked down the opposing leg, its extended paw reaching across the top of his foot. A small constellation of five-pointed stars appeared to twinkle at his neck.

Duke knew the artistry didn't end there. From their tumbles together in the early days of 3-D, he'd gotten intimate with the skull tattooed on the top of the dude's shaft. When Joe-Kev's bone snaked out, thickest in the middle, the skull swelled and stretched with it, flashing a sinister Halloween grin.

Their drummer joined Shaye in the makeup chairs. Arif wandered back in and took his seat. The usual banter filled the air, and a wave of nostalgia embraced Duke. By all outward signs, there had been many blessings associated with being the son of a rock legend. And a legend in his own right, lead singer and stud of a powerhouse coming into its own, this generation's U2 or Electric Light Orchestra. Bigger blessings, like the fame, the fortune and, yes, all that fucking. But it was this little moment, seeing the guys get painted, that he hoped he remembered best when it was over.

And it would be over after this night.

Regret replaced the brief flicker of happiness.

A hand touched his shoulder. Duke seized in place. Turning, he faced Perry, 3-D's lead makeup artist.

"Whoa, dude," Perry said. "Didn't mean to spook you like that. Forgive the pun, but you look like a fucking ghost."

"Sorry, nerves," Duke said.

The other man aimed a thumb toward the lone empty makeup chair. "You ready to become 'Duke De Morte'?"

"*Duke of Death*," Duke sighed, punctuating the statement with a humorless chuckle.

His emerald-colored eyes drifted back toward the guys, each man presently having his face painted into character. The nostalgia was gone completely. More importantly, so was Duke's sense of regret.

"Not yet, man," Duke said, clapping a hand on Perry's arm. "Meet me in my dressing room, would you? And do me a favor. Bring some extra paint with you."

The gimmick sounded lame on the surface at first but had caught on with the fans, especially the legions jerking off to vampire romance novels. The white faces looked elegant, more so when you factored in the crisp white button-down shirts, thin black ties, black suit coats, and shiny black shoes. Total sharpness—and those white ghost faces sure rocked when you shined a black light on them, picking up the phosphorescence on four handsome 3-D apparitions gyrating on stage.

The ghostly faces of 3-D had become as recognizable in recent years as the symbol for the Artist Formerly Known as Prince and Mick Jagger's lips.

Perry finished working on Duke's visage. Duke gazed into the mirror. The work was, as usual, artistry at its purest.

"What do you think?"

Duke studied the perfect glowing white skull painted over his handsome face, his dark hair, a messy but intentional thatch of cowlicks and spikes, his full lips, the lower slightly plumper than its twin on top. Those eyes were so green in the fake skull's sockets that they glowed preternaturally like a wild nocturnal animal's reflecting in a car's headlights.

"I'd fuck me," Duke said.

"Yeah, you and millions of rock junkies around the globe," Perry said.

And Perry knew; they'd enjoyed the occasional fuck since the night that first smear of white face paint went on.

To enhance the look, the guys' suits also reacted to the black light, transforming into an illusion of zombie rags thanks to the invisible chemicals painted onto them by the band's wardrobe department. At intermission, 3-D did a change into kilts, black and white tartan, thick black wool socks, combat boots, and black tuxedo jackets over white shirts. During that fifteen-minute interlude when the opening act, some dude who'd won *Idol* two seasons back, entertained the crowd, the white skulls got a solid touchup.

The four men huddled offstage. Autopsy, his face streaked with intricate red strips of flesh on one side, extended his hand, palm side down. Bones clapped his hand over Autopsy's. Scalpel tossed his mitt onto the pile. The persona known as Duke De Morte hesitated. The other characters, each demanding that their preconcert tradition be maintained, shot him looks.

Duke slammed his hand onto the top of the pile. "*3-D on one... two... three—*"

The four musicians barked the band's name and, as one, raised their hands toward the ceiling. The announcer trilled their arrival over the speakers, and the crowd outside, some ten thousand souls deep, collectively screamed. Duke's cock twitched, a sure sign that he'd gotten hard as he always did whenever the band played to a packed venue. His erections had also become part of the 3-D lore; crotch shots and camera phone video of his tented pants littered the Internet. At last count, according to Harley, there were over fifty thousand amateur websites devoted solely to his dick.

The guys raced onto the scallop-shaped stage ahead of him. More shrieks from their worshippers rose up, and he wondered if the concerts, not the eruption of some volcano, had taken bragging rights to the loudest sound event ever recorded in human history. His ears would ring for days. Duke's nuts tightened against the root of his cock in anticipation. Once he started singing and sweating, they would loosen and spill down his pant legs, hanging, he sometimes imagined, all the way to his hairy ankles.

Steeling himself, Duke pursued. Fuck Vesuvius, the voice in his head decided. The roar that rose up as he trotted toward his Fender guitar was powerful enough to crack the fabric of time and space, to send planets spinning out of orbit and whole constellations of stars crashing into one another.

His cock pulsed.

The audience went insane.

That kind of power, Duke already knew, was dangerous. It could create the universe. But it could also destroy it.

They opened with "Guillotine Romance," their anthem from the teen slasher flick, *Spinal Column*, a gore-fest about the vengeful skeleton of a high school newspaper reporter murdered by fellow students he'd dug up serious dirt on. Their cover of Bonnie Tyler's "Total Eclipse of the Heart" followed, in which hot female werewolf dancers gyrated and slithered to the smoky, liquid melody. From there, it was a catalog of their greatest hits.

"DO *WHAT*?" ASKED Perry.

"You heard me," Duke said. "And be quick about it. We're back on in less than twelve minutes."

Duke's cock was still hard. Not merely stiff, but dripping precome like a leaky faucet. Perry lowered between Duke's spread legs.

"I'll need to clean this off first," he said, licking at Duke's gummed-over slit.

Perry then sucked the head and several inches of shaft between his lips. He tickled Duke's sweating balls. It took everything Duke had to separate from Perry's sucking mouth.

"No, I can't bust right now, and if you keep that up—"

"Yeah, I can see that," Perry said, licking his lips. "Okay, let's do this."

Perry applied the white paint with his fingers, and Duke shuddered, aware of every stroke.

THE BAND RETURNED to the stage dressed in their kilts to a crowd growing hoarser but no less enthusiastic. The regular stage lights followed them through live versions of "Daily Grays," "The Antique Bronze Horse," "Modern Orpheus," and "Violence For Fun and Profit." Then the band launched into its top ten hit, "Surreal Lullaby," which transitioned into a smooth, jazzy take on "Europa."

Shaye abandoned the keyboard for the sax for this particular offering. The lights changed; the eerie luminescence lit their faces. Duke Dalton made his move to center stage, dropped the guitar, and lifted his kilt.

His cock, hard and coated in white paint, snapped up, glowing magnificently. Air, hot with the breaths of devoted fans gusted over Duke's balls, tickling them like a knowledgeable lover's caresses. Legs spread, one arm cast behind his lower back, Duke began to masturbate.

"Go big or go home," he said aloud.

The roar of the crowd swallowed his voice.

Half closing his eyes, spurred on by the frenzied shrieks of his legions of fans who'd quickly caught on to what they were witnessing, Duke choked up on the base of his cock and glided his fingers upward, to just beneath the head. Back down and then up again, he settled into a steady rhythm and dreamed.

Dreamed about Harley's kisses, scattered over his balls and the underside of his shaft, on the tour bus, between one city or another. The road drummed beneath the bus's wheels in his memory. Shaye sleeping in the bed directly across from them, completely oblivious, snoring away, a hand tucked into his underwear and his cock struggling against its imprisonment.

He thought about Joe-Kev and the hunger that had led them to cross the line between bandmates and friends and into the very gray territory of fuck buddies, while backstage after their first gig in LA when they were the opening band, not the star attraction. Duke had never licked a man's ass before. Joe-Kev's was hairy and its sweaty tang had lain heavily on his tongue, disgusting him for all of maybe two seconds. Then he'd feasted upon it, a starving man, and licking ass had become the main course at every sexual buffet since.

There'd been so many moments of great sex, all over the world. But there'd never been love.

He didn't even love the music anymore, if he ever had, which was the true problem and the reason he did it.

Duke unwound his arm behind his back and gripped his balls, an action that made his toes curl in his boots. He couldn't remember them ever feeling this full, this loose.

The notion of escape had freed them beyond their usual bloated state. His cock, too, pulsed with frightening energy. The flashes of camera phones and the telltale sparkles of video applications ignited in the space between his half-open eyelids. Before sunrise, he would be the top entertainment story across the globe, his jerk off routine plastered everywhere you looked on the web.

It would be the end of his career but the start of his life.

That thought pushed Duke over the precipice. Right as the regular lights came on and the spotlights zeroed in on him, Duke released his balls, gave his dick a final double-handed stroke, and pumped six steady shots of his junk into the front row.

Freedom, he thought, shaking the dregs out of his dick.

Only those members of the crowd who weren't scrambling to catch some of his seed were on their feet applauding, and Duke worried that he'd created a bigger monster on his back instead of an exit strategy.

Track 2

FOR WHATEVER REASON, the image of his first guitar hovered in the sweaty darkness over Seamus's eyes. It was made out of a length of two-by-four, painted a shade of muddy blue. Part of an old fence, he remembered. Fishing line, also blue, was strung between the nails. Strumming on it killed his fingertips, even made them bleed—the first time he'd suffered for his art, and at a very young age. The only music that makeshift instrument produced at first was a miserable whine.

Seamus Whyler thought the old fishing wire guitar had miraculously reappeared in his car. Then he remembered the old man had smashed it to a million pieces against the stone wall he and his brother were forced to build that miserable summer, fifteen years behind him. A mosquito buzzed through the gap at the top of the window. Great. Yet one more bloodsucker eager to feed on his corpse.

He stretched out the best he could, his big feet snagging on the brake pedal. A burst of red lit the darkness as the brake lights reflected against the windows of the garage he'd parked in front of. Blood. A running theme of late. Seamus snorted a humorless laugh. Of late? Music was in his blood, and he'd been spilling blood in its honor since that day when, as an eleven-year-old boy, he'd smashed his thumb with a hammer while trying to bang roofing nails into a chunk of broken fence so he could string some fishing line to build a guitar. That would, weeks later, lead to being pummeled by his dad's fists once the old man caught him plucking at it with aching fingers when he was supposed to be building a stone wall to replace the rotting fence.

Seamus had bled for music since.

Sighing, he rolled over, as much as the car seat permitted. His dick sat half hard in his underwear, tempting him to yank it out and forget his worries, at least for all of fifteen minutes. How many days in the past had he strung those fifteen-minute sessions together, one after another? Whole days devoted to masturbating in order to avoid the truth.

The mosquito whined past his ear. He swatted at it and then reached for his baseball cap, sitting on the passenger's seat on top of his present guitar. His fingers brushed the strings, and a rapid-fire succession of memories flooded through his consciousness, channeled through that connection of flesh to chord.

Playing in the high school band, he'd won a shitty talent contest, which hadn't been so big a deal when you factored in the competition. But it had fueled his belief in a music career. A rock star. He was unstoppable.

A college band after that, a few local gigs—weddings and a block party here and there. Then he'd met Wanda Cofield, and their brief time together had meant holding down a steady job—at a warehouse. The Fates might as well have lined him up against the nearest brick wall and opened fire.

That might have been the best and most merciful solution, thought the critic inside Seamus's head. Life since the warehouse, where he drove a forklift and picked orders, had been one miserable letdown after another, tonight's debacle only the latest in a very long string. He'd opted to split the door with the owner of Coralline, a watering hole on the outskirts of Concord. The door, all the soft drinks he wanted—and probably his choice of ass, too, because few could resist the charm of a rock star, even the smallest in the galaxy.

He knocked down three Cokes with lemon and a soda water between sets. The door had netted him a whopping thirty-three bucks plus change. The ass... well, at least living in his car spared him the awkward silence that usually followed a night of anonymous screwing, though it cost him the chance to shower and sleep in a real bed.

Yup, he told that critic inside his skull, Seamus Whyler sure had suffered for his art.

The car was starting to smell like his sweat. A bag of dirty clothes in desperate need of laundering didn't help. He would attend to that on his way south to the Casino Club in Bay Breeze, New Hampshire, where he was booked to play two sets. Bay Breeze was a beach community, but the Casino Club was the sort of place frequented by old money—emphasis on *old*—and itchy young women in search of old money husbands. The mood there was one level of Hell up from the usual. Celebrity musicians in the twilights of their careers played Bay Breeze in the summer. On the drive down, that fact sunk in. The voice in Seamus's thoughts wondered if life had somehow lost its sparkle.

He shot a look toward the passenger's seat, where his regular traveling companions sat. Seamus had hocked the beat-up guitar twice that summer alone. He had only gotten it back from the pawn shop, whose owner was growing nastier by the visit, through the rarest streak of luck. Some drunken customer at a club just north of Boston had tipped him with a fifty probably thinking he'd fished out a five-dollar bill.

At least the Casino Club served food, and eating a decent meal was part of the deal. He could even grab a shower there, and he sure needed one.

SEAMUS ARRIVED EARLY. Toby Cosgrove, the talent coordinator, let him into the dressing room backstage hours before he was due to play, probably out of pity.

"Thanks, dude," Seamus said, clapping Toby on the back.

Toby ran an eye quickly down Seamus's six-foot-two frame of muscles, seeing the pinstriped button-down, the khakis, and old Chucks on big feet, then back up, meeting the scruffy face and emerald eyes beneath the baseball cap's bill. *Equal parts handsome and homeless*, Seamus thought.

"You hungry?"

Seamus shrugged. "I could eat."

"I'll send something up. Great to see you again, man."

"You, too," Seamus said.

The two men shook and exchanged one of those manly hugs, delivered at a distance. The life of most musicians was one endless string of couches to crash on and free meals. You took what was offered and were grateful for it.

Seamus sensed Toby's gaze lingering after the hug ended and shifted from one foot to the next. "Something wrong?"

"No, it's just..." Toby shook his head. "Forget it, man. Let me grab you a bite from the kitchen. Sandwiches okay?"

"I'm so hungry, I'd eat my own foot," Seamus said. It wasn't much of an exaggeration—thirty of his thirty-three bucks and change had gone into the gas tank just to make it to Bay Breeze. Thirty hadn't even filled the tank to the top.

Toby gave him a tilt of the chin, that gesture of understanding between males spoken without the need for actual words. Then the other man turned and marched out of the dressing room, but not before casting another glance his way. It was the latest weird twist in a life that was being smothered by the awkward and uncomfortable.

Seamus tried to put it out of his head. He grabbed his backpack, sitting behind his guitar, and fumbled out a fresh pair of jeans, his last clean ones, a black button-down, underwear, and socks. He fished out his toothbrush and toothpaste, a bar of soap, deodorant, and shampoo and somehow carried all of it into the bathroom in one trip.

The famous, infamous, and forgotten had all showered here in the Casino Club's forty-plus year history. Seamus wondered how many musicians had jerked off and deposited their DNA down the drain. He planned to add his to the unofficial sperm bank, his cock still in need of release. This was the last paying gig he had lined up for the next three weeks; fifteen minutes to forget might still his galloping pulse and push his heart out of his throat and back into his chest where it belonged. A hard life, this was. *Life?* Seamus snorted and shook his head, because this wasn't living.

He remembered what she'd said, Wanda, about how his dad had been right in naming him.

"Seamus," he whispered and began to strip. *"Shame us..."*

CLOTHES DROPPED, BEGINNING with his pinstriped button-down. The white T-shirt underneath released the manly smell of his sweat as he peeled it over his head. Seamus sniffed at the lush fur of his armpits. The hair on his chest was thickest across his pecs. A thin line of dark pelt cut him down the middle before taking a circle around his belly button. From there, it was a short drop into his tangle of pubic curls. The one clear benefit of living hard and worrying about where his next meal was coming from was that his body was in the best shape of his adult life. A banging six-pack of abs lurked visibly beneath all that manly fur.

Seamus kicked off his sneakers. The buttery stink of a real man's sweaty socks assailed his nostrils. He unbuckled his belt, unzipped, and pushed down his khakis, baring a pair of hairy legs, muscular without being showy. The last thing to go were his boxer briefs, charcoal-colored, with a rip along one leg almost big enough for a ball to slip through.

He gave his sac a scratch. The musky smell of his nuts joined the rest, creating a potent scent. Seamus's cock thickened. Pumping it up to its fullest hardness, he admired it in the mirror. There was no shame there—his cock measured just past the nine-inch mark. The thick noose of his foreskin added to the image. One of the few things the old man had gotten right was in not allowing his sons to go under the guillotine without their consent. It was a cock to be proud of, with balls hanging underneath to match.

"Maybe I should have gone into the fucking porn biz," he wondered aloud, pumping his erection and loving the way his body looked in the mirror. But he already knew he was cursed for life because he was a musician at heart, and that was that.

HE NEVER MADE it to the shower before the urge possessed him. Cock pulsing, nuts itchy for release, Seamus hawked a wad of spit onto his hand and started masturbating in front of the mirror. The extra drop of lubrication worked wonders with the natural slickness of his foreskin; soon he was dripping precome. Tugging on his balls added another facet to the experience. Seamus's stones were sensitive, but he loved having them played with. Even better, sucked on.

The opportunity for that quickly presented itself: a shiver teased Seamus's spine, the phantom tickle that comes from being watched by another's prying eyes. Turning toward the open bathroom door, he caught sight of Toby hovering outside, looking in. Their eyes met. Toby kept staring. Seamus let him.

"So, that explains it," Seamus growled.

"Explains what?"

"Nothing," Seamus said. Drawing in a deep breath, he kept going. Being watched, even from another dude, unleashed fresh shivers over his flesh, teasing him from his toes to his balls and all the way up to his throat.

"I... uh... food's on the table."

"Thanks," Seamus sighed. Through narrowed eyes, he focused on Toby, waiting at the threshold. "There anything else?"

"Do you want... Can I...?" The questions went unfinished.

The promise of something better than simply rubbing one out unleashed fresh electricity through his flesh. Seamus nodded. "Why the fuck not. Sure, go for it, dude."

The bathroom door creaked fully open and Toby hurried over, dropping to his knees. A warm breath teased the loose meat of Seamus's nuts, exhaled on a happy sigh. The other man's hands wrestled Seamus's cock free from his fingers.

"Foreskin?" Toby gasped. Before Seamus could reply, he added, "Fucking sweet, dude."

Seamus didn't know how *sweet* his dick-sock was. The lips of the last guy who'd gone down on him had tasted salty when they kissed after the fact.

"It is what it is," Seamus said, reaching down and cupping the back of Toby's head. "So why don't you just suck it, buddy."

Toby hesitated. "Please don't let this get around."

Seamus laughed. "Who the hell am I gonna tell? I'm no one, dude. Just a guy with a guitar... and a hard dick."

Toby licked his skin. By the way the other man's tongue worked into the folds, Seamus knew Toby had experience with pleasuring an uncircumcised cock. The temptation to ask more on the subject almost got the better of him—which fading rock star's uncut cock had squirted its seed between the same lips presently humming upon his? But then he remembered the importance of discretion. Fuck it. A decent blowjob, and by all early signs this one had the makings of a beaut, was like a couch to crash on or a free meal. You took them when offered. So Seamus did.

Toby worked his cock and fondled his balls. The dude had no problem taking his load when he nutted, which solved the dilemma of cleaning up any mess. Shooting on the mirror had seemed like the way to go until Toby's throat provided a better option.

Toby rose from his knees. "There was something else," he said, licking his lips.

"Oh yeah?" Seamus wiped the sweat from his brow. If he was fragrant before Toby's blowjob, the perspiration pouring off him now was ripe.

"This guy came around yesterday, asking for you."

Panic jolted through Seamus's post-bust euphoria. "A guy? What did he want?"

"To see you, I guess."

Along with his string of going-nowhere gigs, Seamus had also left behind a long line of creditors. Old utilities, mostly, and one or two former landlords who hadn't hauled his ass into court for back rent only because they didn't know where to find him in order to serve papers.

"What did this dude look like?" Seamus persisted.

"You know, *a dude*. Good-looking, with a goatee. Snakeskin boots. Twenties, I'd guess."

The mystery man didn't sound like any of the money-grubbers nipping at his ass, but that didn't mean jack. The good-looking guy in his twenties could be a lawyer or a bounty hunter. Toby toyed with his balls, which were pulling tight against Seamus's hairy root. Bounty hunter? Jeezus, his imagination was working overtime. Bounty hunters didn't track down dudes who owed a hundred backs to the electric company and two to cable, fucking pay-per-view.

"I hope you don't mind me telling you this," Toby said, oblivious to his worry. "But I always thought you were really hot, man."

Seamus flashed a sad smile. "Hot, yeah, that's me."

"I mean it. You've got the voice, the looks. You got it all."

Seamus laughed. The outburst sounded mad even to his ears.

"You're—"

"Getting stiff again," Seamus interjected. "So why don't you get back down on your knees and show me some respect."

He pushed on Toby's shoulders and, for the next fifteen minutes or so, forgot his troublesome thoughts about the mystery man who'd tracked him down to Bay Breeze.

THE FIRST SET was a decent mix of covers and original songs that he'd penned and performed dating back to his college days. Seamus ended with an acoustic version of the Incubus hit "Drive," and took to the intermission with a muted round of applause. The audience was bigger than he'd anticipated, but Seamus's expectations based upon previous gigs hadn't been all that high, to begin with.

He excused himself for half an hour, long enough to take a leak, grab a bite, and splash some water on his face. Unhooking the guitar strap, he bowed, running an eye across the intimate gathering. There were a few hot babes present, several of whom he knew wanted to fuck him, because a man with a guitar was an intoxicating image, but no good-looking dudes in their twenties. Or their thirties, for that matter.

Seamus cut around to the back of the stage and tromped down the long hallway behind a door marked for employees only until at last reaching the dressing room. He was tired, cranky, and surprisingly horny, despite the two expert hummers Toby had provided.

Halfway to the bathroom, Seamus realized he wasn't alone. A good-looking man in what Seamus guessed to be his twenties stood near the window in a jaunty pose. Arrogant, even. Dude had a goatee and wore snakeskin boots.

"Mister Whyler?"

"Depends," Seamus said. "Who the fuck are you and what are you doing back here?"

The man uncrossed his expensive snakeskin boots and straightened. "I'm hopefully the guy who's gonna offer you the chance of a lifetime. I've got a job you'd be perfect for."

"A job?" Seamus parroted.

"Yes. But first, I need you to show me your dick."

Track 3

SEAMUS BLINKED.

"Maybe I didn't hear what I think you just said."

The goateed man in the snakeskin boots studied him with the expression of someone who's just seen a ghost. "It's incredible."

Seamus folded his arms. "What's incredible is that I'm gonna shove your head up your own ass if you don't get out of here, pronto."

His wide-eyed fan made no move toward the door. "The resemblance, down to the eye color. A perfect match! That hair's a bit of a mess... but a decent cut would bring it into line. Height and weight proportionate, and that face... *wow*," the guy said, as if Seamus wasn't present in the room.

"Did you not hear my threat, dude?"

"Your cock, that's the deal-sealer."

A smile spread across Seamus's mouth, one he imagined looked quite crazy. He balled his hands into fists. "Just what I need, some crazed stalker who's obsessed with my dick."

The young man blinked. "Huh? No, you have this all wrong."

"What I have is a fuck-knuckle sandwich with your name on it. And don't think I won't charge Toby Cosgrove and the Casino Club an extra fee for taking on bouncer duties, dude."

The other man held up his hand. "Calm down. Seriously, it's just that... you could pass for his twin brother." He extended his hand and bridged the remaining distance. "Hey, man. My name is Harley Deveno. I'm the manager and all-around Dude Friday for the lead singer of 3-D. You know the band? White ghost faces, zombie suits."

"Yeah, I know it," Seamus said, not accepting the man's offer of a handshake. "You work for the guy who beat off on stage in Austin last winter?"

"So you heard."

"Who didn't?"

The dude—Harley Deveno, Seamus's inner voice reminded—flashed a tired smile and shrugged, a look that seemed to suggest he'd already traveled there enough times. "Mind if we sit and talk for a minute?"

"I don't have much more than that. I'm due back on stage for another set."

"You can forget the set," Harley said, casting a look at their surroundings. "And playing in shitty little clubs and dressing in rooms that smell like the inside of an old sneaker and sleeping in your car."

Seamus folded his arms and narrowed his gaze. "How do you know about that?"

"I've done my research. I'm very good at what I do."

"So you're the dude who got that Doctor Death guy to pump his prick on stage is what you're saying?"

Harley took one of the lumpy chairs without waiting for an invitation to sit. "No, I didn't. But I knew Duke—it's Duke, not Doctor—was planning something that night. He was feeling at a loose end, sick of the band's success."

"Oh, boo-hoo," Seamus said.

Harley ignored the snipe. "For all the blowback, I can tell you this—3-D's downloads doubled overnight. We're bigger than ever. Duke's plan backfired... in a good way, depending upon how you look at it."

"So why are you here trying to sneak a look at my wang?"

"Duke's not just my boss," Harley answered. "He's also my best friend. Our dads were in a band together, famous one, back in the day."

"Deveno... Deveno... Valdimore Deveno?"

"The one and only. Dear old dad's one of the guys in those music videos with the huge hair and all that makeup who torture the tight-assed high school teacher determined to stamp out their brand of evil rock. A common theme way back when."

Seamus chuckled. "Him and my old man. My father hated those videos. I loved them, but probably just to spite the mean old prick."

Harley glanced at his watch. "I'd love to talk about this more, but since you're due back on stage, I'll cut to the heart of the matter. Or the *dick* of it. 3-D wants you. We need someone who can take over the role of Duke De Morte on stage until the real Duke comes back from his existential crisis. Our ringer needs to be able to sing, and he's got to be hung halfway to the fucking floor."

Seamus unfolded his arms and reached for his zipper. Saying nothing, he fumbled his meat out. Even limp, it was an impressive sight, and he didn't remain soft for long.

Harley's eyes shot fully open. "Whoa, dude. Is that foreskin?"

"It sure the fuck is."

"That might be problematic, since Duke's dick is cut."

"Problematic for you and him, not me. I've never had any complaints."

Harley rose from his seat and approached. "Do you mind?"

"Do I mind *what*?"

"Can I measure it?"

Seamus took a step back. "No."

"It's purely professional, I promise."

Without waiting for permission, Harley knelt and grabbed hold of Seamus's dick, laying it along the back of his free hand. Seamus's thickening manhood slid past the other man's wrist. The way Harley studied his cock, Seamus expected him to suck it.

"Fuck," Harley said, a wide smile on his face. "I want you."

Seamus choked up on his dick like a major leaguer and swung, smacking Harley across the cheek. "Yeah, I see that."

The grand slam left a trace of goo on the side of Harley's face. It also shocked him out of his thoughts and back to the real discussion. "No, you don't understand. I want to hire you. Send you on tour with 3-D. The stage makeup will conceal any doubt, and I know you've got a hell of a set of pipes on you from listening in on your set. You'll be paid handsomely, and there will be plenty of other benefits."

"You're crazy," Seamus said. He struggled to tuck his dick back under cover and saw stars. "Is this some kind of reality TV stunt? Are you trying to punk my junk?"

Harley reached into his back pocket, pulled out his wallet, and produced a business card. "I won't justify that with an answer. You want the gig, call me."

Seamus accepted the card. "You want me to take you seriously, how about you stick around, hear me play, and we'll talk about it after my set."

Saying nothing more, Seamus exited the dressing room. Any desire to eat was gone, and the sliver of belief teasing him that Harley Deveno and his offer were legit quickly evaporated. He played through the next set to a thinning crowd half of what it had been, and the good-looking man with the goatee who'd fondled his dick wasn't part of the audience.

THE FATES WERE fucking with him, the same way they had for years. What were the chances that some big name band needed a pauper to take over the kingdom for their disenfranchised prince, who'd whipped it out and burped it for all the world to see?

Seamus packed up his guitar, polished off the last of a plate of fried fish, shoestring potatoes, and coleslaw that was starting to do backflips in his stomach, and gathered his things.

Toby handed him his check. "The usual."

The usual was two hundred bucks. Seamus pocketed it. The cash wouldn't go far. His nausea worsened.

"You need a place to crash tonight?" Toby asked. "I have a house on the beach, right up the road. You're welcome to come over, hang out."

And get his dick slurped on all night, Seamus thought.

While the concept wasn't without merit, Seamus wanted to drive. Drive until he couldn't go any farther, park the car that had become his only home, and, as was inevitable, suffer. He didn't know how much more he could take before he finally snapped, but Seamus sensed it wasn't that far down the road.

He'd parked in the club's VIP lot. At some point in the night, a black stretch limo had pulled up behind him, blocking him in.

One of the rear windows rolled down as he approached.

"Seamus," Harley said.

While Seamus readied to launch a smart remark at the dude, another window lowered and Seamus found himself staring into a mirror. Only the mirror was alive.

"Why don't you get in the limo," Duke Dalton said. "We've got a lot to talk about."

Seamus leaned into the window. "Duke Dalton. Or should I say Duke De Morte—the man, the myth, the masturbator."

Duke raised his chin in silent acknowledgement and smiled. "Guilty."

Looking at Seamus Whyler was like seeing himself in an out-of-body way. His accidental twin hadn't shaved, and the prickle of scruff coating his chin, cheeks, and throat matched the day's worth on his own face. Their eyes, faces, hair color, all of it was nearly identical. Even the manly scent of Seamus's skin, a mix of clean sweat peppered by excited chemical reactions, was familiar. He'd smelled his sweat after sex and performances on stage; he and Seamus could be twins.

"Incredible," Seamus said. "I'm starting to think this isn't some fucked-up stunt after all. That it could be legit."

"It is," Harley said. "But it isn't something we want the whole world knowing, so if you wouldn't mind getting your fucking ass in the car...."

It was the tone Harley often took with him, but it gave Duke a good laugh to hear it used on the stranger with his face.

"Fine," Seamus grumbled.

Harley opened the door, and Seamus struggled in with his guitar and backpack.

"Drink?" Harley offered, aiming a thumb at the limo's wet bar. "Just so you know, we don't allow alcohol in any of our venues."

"You don't?"

"No. You'll understand why—if you decide you're interested in our offer."

"I'm interested," Seamus said. He eyeballed Duke, disbelief obvious in both of their expressions. "And it's a good idea that I don't hit up the sauce, because when I wake from this dream, I'd like to believe it wasn't a booze-fueled trip."

"It's not." Duke extended his hand. "I can't tell you how happy I am to meet you, dude."

Seamus shook. "Back at you. Happy, and creeped out."

"It's uncanny," Harley said.

Duke nodded. "It's perfect."

"Except for that matter about his dick."

THEY ENTERED THE hotel through a private entrance, riding an elevator up to the thirty-first floor. Downtown Boston spread beneath them. A fruit basket and snacks lined the counter, more food than Seamus had seen in the past two weeks. Bottles of water and soda, too.

"Get you something?" Harley asked.

Duke Dalton answered, "Just a little privacy, pal."

"But—?"

"We'll be okay. I'll shout if Seamus and I need your assistance."

Reluctantly, Harley acquiesced, ducking into one of the suite's three bedrooms. When they were alone, Duke grabbed two water bottles. He tossed one to Seamus, who caught it with an overhand grab.

"Bottom line," Duke said after plunking his butt onto a colorful, modern sofa. "I'm burned out."

"I hear you," Seamus said, sitting across from him. "Fame's such a bitch. All those groupies and Benjamins get so tedious."

Duke shook his head and gazed out the window at the cityscape beyond. "You don't get it."

"You'll pardon me for not getting it, but I've spent the last four months living behind the wheel of my car, eating out of cereal boxes and off dollar menus."

This brought the two mirror images eye to eye. "I've never had that."

"Had what? An empty stomach? Seriously, what are you bitching and moaning about? You poor little rich kid."

"I've had the empty stomach—once. But I've never had to suffer for my art," Duke snapped. "I've never had to fight for it or work for it."

Seamus took an angry swig from his water bottle. "You're not winning me over."

"From my earliest memory, music was a part of my world. I hail from rock royalty, dude... but the music, that actual fucking *melody*, we're strangers."

"So what is it that you really want?"

Duke drew in a deep breath, held it, and then just as deeply released the sigh from his lungs. "I think that living behind the wheel of a car and eating out of cereal boxes and off dollar menus would be great, for a start."

Seamus could tell by the desperate look on his reflected face that the man was serious. Gravely so.

"So what are you suggesting? That we just up and switch places? You'd put yourself through my life sentence?"

"If you walked in my shoes, you'd understand. And I hope you will, because if I don't get out of the spotlight and figure out what really matters, I'm going to snap. Or worse. Be me for a while," Duke pleaded. "Let me be you."

"Me be *you*?" Seamus repeated. "Lead singer for 3-D?"

"The money, the celebrity, all of it," Duke said.

Suddenly and without warning, Seamus felt the corners of his eyes sting with a trace of mist. He hadn't cried in a very long time, not since the old man beat the tears out of him that summer, behind the stone wall. The image of the fishing line guitar flashed before him, projected onto the mist, and he understood the significance—the last time he'd cried had been the day his father broke the guitar beneath his steel-toe boot. He hadn't cried as a result of the beating, but for the music, which was his heart, his soul.

The man sitting across from Seamus was an idiot who'd had every one of his dreams handed to him and resented it.

"You want that life, you got it," Seamus said.

Relief washed over his reflection's face. "*Harley.*"

The other man reappeared. "Yeah, Duke?"

"We have an agreement."

Harley set the contract on the table in front of Seamus.

"Six weeks. You get a million dollars for your time, after the Death Heart 2 tour is over. During the six weeks, you'll have access to an expense account, you'll stay with the band but have private accommodations, and access to Duke's mansion in Beverly Hills between cities. You won't tell anyone about the arrangement. If you do, you forfeit the payout."

Seamus sucked in a deep sip of air, convinced he might pass out at any second. "There's no one to tell."

He moved to sign, but Duke stopped him. "There's one last thing."

"Let me guess—my dick?"

Duke unbuttoned his fly while kicking off his sneakers. "I created something big that night in Austin."

"Yeah, *huge*," Seamus chuckled.

He followed suit and started to strip. The two men studied one another as shirts dropped and socks came off, leaving big feet bare. Pants followed. Duke Dalton stepped out of his underwear. Seamus peeled his down. They faced one another, naked and stiff, full balls hanging loose and low. Seamus's junk had more hair. Duke's toenails, he saw, were neater. Then there was the matter of one reflection's foreskin. Otherwise, they could have been clones.

"Damn," Harley said. "It's a double dose of amazing."

Duke gave his dick a shake. "I'd say that we're a decent match in the cock department, too."

Harley sank to his knees between the two men. "Let me be the judge of that."

Then, before Seamus could protest, Harley gripped their dicks by the root and mashed their heads together between his lips.

Track 4

THE EASE IN which Harley helped himself to the two straining cocks in front of his face made it clear that he and Duke Dalton were more than simply boss and assistant. *More than just good buddies, too*, Seamus thought. The way Harley managed to take Duke's monstrous endowment to the balls without choking suggested he'd gotten plenty of practice over the years. It wasn't their first time in this position; the number was probably somewhere in the thousands.

Harley spit out Duke's cock and then showed a similar skill in swallowing Seamus's down until his nostrils met the dense carpet of pubic curls. Twice earlier in the day, the events coordinator at the Casino Club had played his bone with finesse; now, another dude was making love to his dick, sucking it deep into his throat while toying with his nuts. On paper, the assistant was doing a decent job, conscious to shield teeth and to tickle more than twist his balls. But to Seamus's rising confusion, it wasn't Harley that excited him the most. That honor belonged to his reflection.

Seamus liked jerking off in front of a mirror, seeing his above-average cock and muscular body being worked into a frenzy until the white stuff blasted out, coating the glass. Here, it was like watching a life-sized, living copy, a clone. The intimacy overwhelmed him. Boldly, he reached a hand toward Duke Dalton's shoulder to steady himself. Duke wrapped an arm around his in response, and the connection was electric.

"This is just one of the many benefits of being me," Duke grunted.

Suddenly, his reflection was directly beside his ear, his voice warm against Seamus's skin. That face was so handsome, his scent insanely arousing, pushing chemical receptors into overdrive. Unable to resist, Seamus leaned closer. Duke met him halfway. They nuzzled the sides of their faces together. Prickle scratched against prickle. Lips met at the corners but hastily sought one another full-on. The first kiss was more of a nip. The second was delivered hard to the verge of painful. Open mouths followed, and tongues quickly sought one another.

"Yes," Duke sighed between repetitions.

Seamus breathed in the other man's voice. His *voice now*, he thought, aware from the periphery that Harley had lined up their cockheads and was working his foreskin over Duke's knob, doing magical things with it. The lion's share of his focus was on the good fortune that would greet him with the rising sun—fame and financial freedom, more money than he'd ever be able to spend, and a bona fide taste of the kind of celebrity he'd dreamed throughout his entire life. It didn't matter that it was Duke Dalton's celebrity, or that he was an imposter, a ringer, a golden-throated doppelganger inserted to maintain an illusion. And it wasn't like he was being hired to lip-synch—Seamus Whyler was many things, but he sure as fuck could sing.

He sighed a breathy, "*Fuck*," and Duke drank it in, making the transfer complete. They kissed again, and it was not lost on Seamus that both of them were smiling.

DUKE SMILED.

The invisible weight sitting on his shoulders and spine, crushing him to death, relented without fanfare. A pain he'd been aware of for years wasn't there anymore. What good was a life where everything was handed to you and you had no worries? It sounded idyllic—unless it was your reality, and you had nothing to measure paradise against. A perfect life grew stale and miserable quickly. How could one appreciate all that he had, especially opportunities and open doors, if he'd never worked for them? Gliding effortlessly through life because you were the son of Jack Dalton and, as such, pure rock royalty, born to the throne?

The weight lifted, and something magical happened to Duke's dick.

He glanced down through the tangle of limbs, his and Seamus Whyler's, to see Harley carefully rolling the other man's lush sock of foreskin over his straining dickhead. Seamus's noose engulfed his crown fully and even managed to cover a fraction of an inch of shaft. The illusion of one giant cock, connecting both men above their balls, captured his gaze. The weight was gone from Duke's spine and shoulders; the fresh pressure squeezing Duke's cock was glorious, unlike anything he'd ever experienced before.

"What the fuck are you doing, dude?" Seamus asked.

"Little trick I picked up along the way. They call it 'docking,'" Harley said.

He gave their dicks, now joined at the heads, a pump from each shaft. Duke moaned something unintelligible between Seamus's open lips. As one, the two men rose to the tops of their toes. This allowed Harley easier access to their balls.

One at a time, Duke's nuts vanished into his good buddy's maw. The clean, animalistic smell of male sweat rose up to tease his nostrils. He was free.

"Thank you," Duke said.

His eyes drew Seamus's into their gravitational pull.

"Yeah, you, too, man."

They kissed again, and the pressure of Seamus's moist foreskin gliding back and forth over their cockheads drove him over the edge. Duke fired first, his heightened consciousness aware of the incredible sensation as his shots of come ricocheted off the inside of Seamus's cock-sock, filling the tube.

Seamus's howls joined his, as did his reflection's fresh blasts inside their joined dicks. The warmth and wetness was, Duke mused, the most intimate connection he'd ever known. He didn't want it to end and resented that Harley worked Seamus's foreskin away, separating their tools, there to lap up the flood of mingled skeet that poured out.

Seamus stepped back. Like their dicks, arms unlaced, leaving only the sweat glistening on their chests, the masculine stink in the air, and Harley's wet lips as proof of what had happened.

"That was fucking great," Duke said.

Seamus gave his dick a shake and his nuts a hearty scratch. "Dude, *great* doesn't begin to do it justice."

"You call this justice?" laughed Harley, still on his knees, a slop of come congealing on his face.

If not for the awesome trick utilizing his extra length of skin, Seamus might have forgotten their twosome was really comprised of three.

Harley tugged at his own erection through his jeans. Seamus took a step back.

"Pal, I don't roll that way," said Seamus.

"What way is that?"

"You know."

Harley shook his head. "No, I don't. And neither do you."

Standing, he gripped each reflection's cock, both still partially hard, and walked them toward the nearest bedroom.

The morning would break with new promise, Seamus knew. Perhaps the freedom from worry about finances and failure was the driving force keeping his nuts loose and his dick stiff. It didn't hurt matters that he was also enjoying some of the best sex of his life on the night before the highly anticipated sunrise, his inner critic chided.

This latest round started off as a playful shoving match, with Duke tackling him onto the bed. There, the two men wrestled, grinding swords. Harley's mouth sought Seamus's balls. Before long, his cock and his reflection's returned to standing at full hardness.

While Harley stripped, revealing a tight, slender body that was mostly smooth from the waist up apart from armpits and a thin treasure trail of chestnut hair, and carpeted from the crotch down to his ankles, Seamus's mind wandered.

Just hours before, he was sitting on stage at the Casino Club, strumming his guitar, not knowing where to go next or *if* there'd be a sunrise. That life could change so quickly unleashed a shudder down his sweaty spine. What if he'd actually snapped and everything taking place around him in the suite's master bedroom was a figment of his addled brain?

Seamus closed his eyes. Fear kept them shut for several long, tense seconds. Then he felt a warm mouth on his cock. Looking again, he saw Harley between his spread legs and his reflection stretched out beside him. The reflection reached up and cupped his cheek. Their eyes met. This was real.

"Stay there," Duke growled to Seamus.

Seamus shrugged. Fine. As he lay on his back enjoying the surprises as they unfolded, Duke eased to the foot of the bed. There, Seamus watched the man with his face maneuver between Harley's legs, spreading the cheeks of his ass apart. Flashing a devilish grin that was only visible for a moment, Duke dipped closer and licked. The wet sucking sounds that rose up spurred Seamus's excitement nearly as much as the way Harley's mouth worked over his dick.

Yes, life sure was fucking strange. The start of a new song played through his thoughts, something about tasting Hell before you could fully appreciate Heaven. He doubted he'd forget the words, though the heavenly aspect came right as he was thinking about reaching into the nightstand drawer for paper and pen.

Ironically, Harley straddled him to do just that, only he pulled out a pair of foil packets. Seamus glanced down. Duke's mouth was wet and shiny, curled into a lusty smile.

"You're gonna fucking love this, dude," Duke said.

Harley tossed a condom to his reflection and then tore open the second, rolling it over Seamus's head and down his shaft. Harley then climbed on top of him and, he assumed, it was Duke who gripped him by the root, lining the tip of his dick with Harley's well-licked hole.

This Seamus wasn't sure about. Having a skilled set of lips work wonders on you was one thing. Spearing another dude up the ass—

Whatever protest he might have made died as he slipped in and a tightness unlike anything he'd ever experienced engulfed his cock. If penetrating Harley's asshole was the best and tightest fuck he'd ever rocked, it only held the top position for a matter of seconds, the record shattered when Duke rose up from between Harley's legs, his intention clear.

Harley moaned, the pained smile on his face far past happy, in a state of complete euphoria. He licked his lips, his tongue traveling the circumference around his trim goatee. Duke leaned over the middleman's shoulder, and Seamus saw a similar joy written in his expression. Something thick and hard squeezed past his cock in Harley's ass, and Seamus almost bucked the weight of the two men off the bed in the rush of pleasure that washed through him.

The underside of Duke's cock rubbed his, and Harley's tightness clamped down on both men's dicks, again linking them together.

Seamus imagined the look on his face mirrored theirs.

Duke drew back and then pushed in. A blue streak of expletives flew past Seamus's lips. The brush of Duke's hairy legs against his, the warm puddles of flesh bouncing together that were their four, fat balls, and the manly scent in the room soon left him clutching at the bedclothes, driven mad by the combination of Harley's asshole and Duke's stabbing cock.

Unable to resist, Seamus reached up and seized hold of Harley's face. Drawing it down to his, he channeled his aggression into a kiss, his taste and Duke's heavy on the other man's lips. If he never had sex again, this would be going out on top, Seamus thought. Something told him that double-stuffing Harley's ass was only a taste of the fun to follow in his exciting new world.

Lyrics and refrains passed through his mind. Whole arias and operas, all while the pressure built and Duke's dick rubbed him closer to unloading. Fuck, how quickly life could change! For once, it had swung in a happy direction. A million bucks... he could buy a new car, a house... or just stick the money in a sock... a hundred socks... and continue to play his music without worry about living on the edge of disaster for the rest of his life.

The music inside his skull crescendoed. His body reacted, and his cock began to shoot.

"I'm coming!" Seamus moaned around Harley's mouth.

The dick stabbing up and down against his seemed to double in size. "Oh, fuck, me, too," Duke growled.

Not to be left out, Harley attended to his own needs by rubbing one out against Seamus's six-pack and painted his midriff in whitewash.

Then, one at a time, their bodies untangled.

A dream?

Seamus lurched awake in the broken shadows before dawn, again doubting that the events of the past eight or so hours had actually taken place. The ache in his nuts, which felt like they'd been drained dry, and the luxurious comfort beneath his spine proved otherwise. Seamus hadn't slept in a real bed, let alone one as magical as this, in ages. Since the winter's cold broke and spring arrived, his bed had been the front seat of his car, the occasional sofa, and the rare one-night stand. Those beds never felt comfortable.

Seamus scratched his balls, which were the most telling testimony to the fact that this morning would break differently from every other preceding dawn. His cock lay half-stiff over his stomach. He gave it a handshake. Masturbating behind the wheel of a parked car in the daylight was almost as dangerous as performing the same act while traveling at sixty-five down the highway. Seamus loved jerking off only slightly less than he loved a good hum job.

He could beat his dick for hours here, in the comfort of a real bed; could blast as much of his batter into the mattress as he wanted to without worry. Or as little, his inner critic reminded, because his nuts had pumped out what felt like a gallon of cream since his arrival to Boston.

Seamus cast a look toward the windows. The trio of six-foot panes facing the same patch of cityscape as the great room showed the lights of the skyscrapers set against a moody patch of darkness. The sun hadn't yet risen; when it did, the day would break overcast according to the reports he'd heard on the radio in his car, in that other life.

He continued to fondle his dick, but it was really a background jerk, out of habit. His mind raced. Today, everything was due to change.

The panic set in.

He tore back the covers and lurched up from the bed. His car—it was still parked outside the Casino Club. No great loss when you considered in six week's time, he'd be a millionaire. But as destitute as his life had grown, there were still priceless elements in it, like his scrapbook. And the scrapbook was in the trunk of his car.

Cock still swollen and demanding attention, Seamus found his boxer briefs, discarded at the side of the bed, and pulled them on. He padded to the bedroom door, opened it. Duke stood at the windows, dressed in underwear and a T-shirt, staring at the city, silently contemplating who-knew-what.

Their eyes met. "Hey," Seamus said.

Duke answered with a tired smile that looked sad at the edges. "Morning."

"Yeah, so it is. Hey, I was just thinking that I need to get back to Bay Breeze."

Duke gave his package a squeeze. "Why's that?"

"My car, my stuff."

"That's *my* stuff for the next six weeks."

Seamus straightened. His face turned to stone. "Come again?"

"You're me, I'm you, remember?"

"Yes, but—"

"Don't worry. I'll keep an eye on your life until you return to it. You do the same to mine."

Seamus exhaled. "Would you do me a huge favor?"

"Sure."

"In the trunk, in a leather attaché… there's a scrapbook. I've kept it since I played my very first gig. There's a matchbook or cocktail napkin from every single place I've ever made music. It's the one thing I have besides my music that I love. Keep it safe, would you?"

Duke Dalton fixed him with a deep, unsettling gaze.

"What?" Seamus asked.

"That's so… completely fucking awesome. Your scrapbook. Wow," he said. "I'll guard it with my life."

"Thanks. Anything you want me to take extra-special care of?"

"No," Duke said. "Nothing at all."

Over the other man's shoulder, Seamus noticed the sky had gradually lightened. Dawn was breaking through in muddy strokes.

Harley emerged from the third bedroom, completely naked, his slender dick bobbing stiffly with his steps. Seamus remembered how Toby had described him: goateed, good-looking. For the first time, just how attractive the man was sank in.

"Hey, I heard voices," Harley said, stretching. His dick flounced. "I'll order up some coffee."

As he passed Seamus, Harley dug in his heels, clapped a hand to Seamus's bare chest, and pecked a kiss to his cheek.

"Good morning, *Duke*," Harley said.

Seamus smiled. It sure was. Hands down, the best fucking morning of his life!

Track 5

WATER CASCADED DOWN his body, hot and invigorating. Duke half-expected Harley to wander into the suite's standup shower, wash his back, eat his ass, and plunge down on him, one farewell suck-job to sustain him until they met again, on the other side. Only his good buddy didn't, leaving him to his own measures. While lathering his dick, Duke figured that Harley sensed his need for privacy. It was time to wash away the old life in readiness for the new.

Duke started to masturbate. Images flashed through his thoughts, only they weren't the sort that he suspected. Instead of Harley's insanely tight asshole or talented lips, or the endless parade of sweaty, choice flesh there for the taking in his everyday world, he thought about the scrapbook.

What a brilliant concept. It made the platinum records hanging on the walls of his studio in Beverly Hills seem pale in comparison. A scrapbook containing matchbook covers and cocktail napkins was intimate proof of the purest love. Visualizing it sent his balls low and quickly brought his erection to the point of climax. He'd never been in love before. The emotion overwhelmed him, and he busted his seed down the drain thinking he'd been baptized after a fashion, blessed with new hope.

Duke toweled dry and reached for the fresh set of briefs and socks sitting on the counter then hesitated.

"No," he said, shaking his head.

Duke glanced into the fogged-over mirror. His reflection hovered out of focus behind a sheen of steam, his face that of a ghost. Dark emotion threatened to smother his hopefulness. But hadn't he always been a ghost, a shadow? Living in the shadow of Jack Dalton and Stage Fright first and then behind the white makeup and mask of Duke De Morte and 3-D.

He wiped a hand across the mirror. His face partially appeared among the smear of water drops. Duke Dalton had always been a shadow—was transforming into Seamus Whyler such a big stretch?

Transformation. Grabbing his briefs and socks, he marched out of the bathroom, his cock swinging. Seamus and Harley were showered and dressed, enjoying room service breakfasts and robust-smelling coffee. Another plate sat under a silver cloche, waiting for him.

"Put that thing away, dude, before you poke someone's eye out," Seamus said lightly, aiming his fork at Duke's dick.

"I can't, not yet," Duke answered. He studied the man with his face, saw that he was wearing the same shirt and jeans, the same beat-up and well-traveled sneakers from the previous night's late adventures. "You need to strip."

A cocky smirk swept over Seamus's face. He fondled the bulge at the front of his pants. "Thanks, man, but I'm spent. Seriously."

"No, you're not reading me. I'm you now, and you're me." Duke tossed his designer underwear and socks. Seamus caught them in his free hand. "*You* in every way, and that includes your clothes, walking in your shoes."

Seamus's grin sagged. "Are you serious?"

Duke didn't answer with words, the look on his face telegraphing that he was. Resigning himself to the inevitable, Seamus stood, kicked off his shoes, and worked on undoing his belt.

"Okay, if you're that hardcore about this whole thing, but I gotta warn you, those shoes...they've logged plenty of wear and are fairly ripe, dude."

Duke didn't comment. Seamus stripped off his socks, jeans, finally his underwear. Balling them up, he pitched his boxer briefs at Duke. Duke caught them with the same effortless skill, detecting the scent of soap and balls. Without hesitation, he pulled them on. By the time he donned Seamus's socks and jeans and was buttoning his shirt from the bottom up, he'd ceased being Duke Dalton and was somebody else.

Seamus eased into the other man's underwear and then his socks, a new pair, brand name that came up only to the ankles. Duke handed him a tracksuit, stylish, expensive. Baseball cap and shades and new cross trainers completed the picture. Seamus mentally calculated that the entire ensemble was likely worth more than his car.

"How much do you have in your wallet?" Duke asked.

Seamus tipped him a look. "Why?"

Duke reached into his pocket and pulled out his billfold. "Here's mine. Now give me yours."

Seamus glanced into the billfold. The thing was stuffed. He figured the bills weren't singles. "About two hundred bucks," he said, reaching for his, which sat beside his basic, prepaid cell phone on one of the suite's side tables. "But that's hardly a fair exchange."

"Fair or not, it's the deal. Your cell, too."

Seamus handed his wallet and shitty cell phone to the man wearing his underwear and face. "Here you go."

"You'll have Duke's cell," Harley said, studying the exchange with interest. "It's a private number. Only the members of the band know it."

"What about your dad?" Seamus asked.

The temperature in the room plummeted.

"My dad?"

Seamus glanced at Harley before answering. The young man's lusty grin at seeing them strip and transform was gone.

"Well, sure. What if he calls or, you know, stops by to see you but instead finds me?" Seamus stammered.

"That won't happen," Duke said, stone-faced. "I don't see my father anymore. Neither will you."

Seamus opened his mouth, intending to comment, only to again clamp it shut. Whatever had passed between the Dalton men, father and son, was dark territory best left unexplored by strangers.

"You'll see the band and Perry, our lead makeup artist. During the time of the contract, you'll be shielded from the media. The white-mask you'll wear on stage should fool everyone else," Harley said. "My only concern, as previously stated, is that beautiful dick of yours."

"My dick?" Seamus snorted. "It didn't seem to concern you too much when it was lodged in either end of you last night."

"Let me rephrase—your *foreskin*. The point is, Duke's dick is cut. I'm wondering how I'm going to explain that to the first music journalist or blogger who wants to know how Duke Dalton suddenly sprung a noose of cock-sock around his wiener."

Seamus folded his arms. "And why would any of them be staring at my wiener, dude? You don't mean...?"

"Yes, he does," Duke said.

"After Duke gave that hot solo performance in Austin to "Europa," it's expected that he's gonna do it again. Ticket sales for 3-D have always been most excellent, but Death Heart 2 sold out in less than an hour, and you can probably guess why. There are fans out there that would trade their internal organs for the chance to be in the front row and catch a wad of Duke De Morte's baby-juice across the cheek. Lots of them."

"You expect me to jerk off in front of a stadium full of crazed concert-goers, just like that?"

"No, we expect Duke Dalton to," Harley said. "So if you want out, now's your last chance."

Seamus contemplated what was at stake. Apparently, so had his cock, which stood out thickly in his new tracksuit pants. "Fuck, no," he sighed, raising his hand in a high five.

Duke met it, and the two men embraced.

"Take care of my fans," Duke said, kissing the side of his cheek.

"You take care of my scrapbook."

"Promise."

Seamus clapped the other man's back, aware of the press of their mutually hard cocks together and his scent, on his clothes, male and strangely erotic as it emanated off the body of his reflection. Hugging Duke was like grinding dicks with himself.

"Thanks, man," Duke sighed. "I hope this doesn't sound too weird, but I'm starting to care for you like the twin brother I never had."

"Dude, I passed weird last night, right around the time the two of us stuck our dicks into the same hole at the same time. But I feel the way you do—maybe *because* we stuck our dicks into the same hole at the same time."

He kissed Duke's cheek. Their mouths soon connected, and the sensation was intensely erotic, curiously comfortable. Anything sexual that had happened between them seemed as natural as masturbation, like nutting while staring at his reflection in the mirror.

Duke reached down and fondled Seamus's cock through the nylon material of his pants. Seamus moaned around his reflection's lips. Duke's tongue slipped in.

Seamus closed his eyes and savored the raw yet effortless emotion. To his surprise, it took little prodding for him to grope Duke's dick. It pulsed and pushed against his fingers through the worn denim of his old blue jeans, which were starting to fray at the cuffs and just below where his balls hung. He reached for the zipper. That nifty docking trick, he felt sure he could reproduce it on his own this time, though he figured Harley would be there in a heartbeat for the chance to get the two men off and clean up the mess.

Then Duke's hand covered his, guiding it away from zipper and cock. "No, dude."

"Why?"

"Because if you do, I'll never leave. I'll never get out of here. I'll never..." He grunted something in Seamus's ear that sounded like, "... *live*."

Then Duke rested his cheek flush against Seamus's, and Seamus nuzzled against his reflection, loving the connection. A final deep kiss, full on the lips, and Duke broke their embrace.

Saying nothing, he pocketed Seamus's cell phone, adjusted his crotch, and started toward the door.

"Hey, wait," Harley said.

Harley jumped off the sofa. Duke dug in his heels and turned. The two men embraced. Duke, easily fifty pounds more than Harley's body mass and half a foot taller in height, lifted his buddy off his feet.

"I'll be okay," Duke said.

"You'd better—or else!"

Duke smacked Harley's ass. "I expect to find this as tight as when I left. I'll send the driver back for you dudes after he drops me off in Bay Breeze." "Why don't we all ride up together, and then Seamus and I can hop over to the airport?"

"I'm Seamus now," Duke said. "But sure, yeah, I'd like that. You've got five to gather your stuff."

Duke spanked Harley's ass again, this time hard enough to produce a small thunderclap. Harley bitched about the treatment, but not too seriously. Not long after that, they were all seated in the rear of the limo, driving through the moody gray morning.

Duke exited the limo. Seamus tossed him the car keys through the open door. The goodbyes were brief, delivered in an economy of words. Then Harley told the limo driver to head for the airport where, Seamus learned, Duke Dalton's private jet sat parked and waiting for them. Next stop Los Angeles.

Duke closed the limo door and turned toward the car, whose windshield showcased the first trace of raindrops. As the limo drove away, Seamus had the strange sense that he was staring at himself from outside his own body, watching his physical form standing in the rain, fumbling with his car keys, facing an uncertain future.

The image was fleeting. They turned onto Route 1 and were soon speeding along the coast, and Seamus wasn't Seamus anymore, a musician one short step ahead of disaster. He was Duke Dalton, mega-rich, a man with his own private jet, a man who lived in a world of top-shelf luxuries and room service ordered at hotel suites. A man living *the life.*

He shot a look at Harley and sniffed the air, catching the barest hint of the cologne he'd spritzed on in his haste to exit the hotel on time. Seamus's dick twitched. He grabbed at his crotch, flashed a cocky smirk, and said, "Get the fuck over here."

Harley reached for a button and pushed it. The privacy screen between the back of the limo and the driver rolled up. Then, matching Seamus's grin with one of his own, Harley sank to his knees between Seamus's feet. Wasting no time, Harley eased down his track pants and the designer underwear. Duke's underwear.

He was Duke now.

Leaning back, Seamus savored the neat, easy maneuvers Harley made—freeing his dick, tugging on his balls, licking at his foreskin and obviously loving its taste and scent, if the joy on his face was any indication.

Harley sucked his dick as the limo drove on toward the private jet. Seamus had a wallet filled with hundred-dollar bills and credit cards. By nightfall, his head would sink into a comfortable pillow on a bed that would be the equivalent of sleeping on a cloud.

Over the next six weeks, his meals would be exquisite, the finest gourmet dining. He would play as the front man in one of the most famous bands in the business. He'd be a million dollars richer when all was said and done. And the availability of hot, instant sex like the kind he was presently enjoying boggled the mind.

The dream was his!

"Suck my cock, you hot little fucker," Seamus said.

He thought about reaching down and grabbing the back of Harley's head, guiding him up and down, but realized he didn't have to. He was rock royalty now. He was Duke Dalton. That goatee knew exactly what was expected of it.

Seamus tucked both arms behind his head and reclined in the pose of lazy men receiving the greatest head of their lives. This felt like the best.

"Oh yeah, dude," he growled. "Suck it."

A gust of humid air rippled around Duke, rotten with the smell of the garbage in the nearby dumpster and the ocean's brine. With its windows rolled up, Seamus's car had bottled the stink of a man's sweat along with old fast food wrappers and the dirt tracked in on the treads of damp shoes.

The contents of Seamus Whyler's life were stacked on the back seat and, he knew with a rising sense of excitement, stored in the trunk. Duke popped the latter and found the leather attaché. More importantly, the scrapbook stored inside. It was a big, gangly book with a green faux-leather cover and stiff pages. Sitting behind the wheel, Duke gave it a cursory scan. Dozens of cocktail napkins, matchbook covers, and dates sprawled in magic marker flipped past, proof of a life lived in honor of love.

Love for the muse, for *music*.

Duke realized he'd gotten hard beneath the scrapbook's spine and reached a hand down to adjust his cock. The unpleasant odors outside the car mixed with the ones inside, all punctuated by the crisp scent of the scrapbook.

This is how music really smells, Duke thought. The sweat and the sadness, the small victories and the sparkles of persistent hope. He drew in a deep breath and reached beneath his belt. Among the stink of rainy parking lots and stale sweat socks was another, that of a man's seed. Duke imagined Seamus jerking off behind the wheel, late at night, from one parking lot to the next. His cock pulsed beneath his hand. The voyeuristic thrill of examining another man's life intensified before crackling out.

These were his things now, at least until he found his way back to his old life. It struck him as he reached his other hand lower to unzip his pants that, crazy as it sounded, he might not want to relinquish Seamus Whyler's identity. The skin fit him so comfortably. He liked this little compact world, a world devoted solely to one mission, one love. Music.

As Duke tugged at his zipper, someone knocked on the window.

Track 6

THE IDEA CAME to him during the early morning hours, when his mind drifted and his ass hurt, despite the comfortable seat cushions. A lot of him ached, for that matter—his legs, his neck and shoulders, especially his balls, which hung bloated and sweating in his black limousine driver's pants, aching for release. Patrick Karser pumped one off just after 2:00 a.m., thinking about the cute little goateed cock-knocker who'd hired him. In the fantasy, Patrick had the dude bent over the hood doggy-style and was sticking it to him without mercy. Privileged little puke. Things verged on violence. And then he came into the napkin he'd fished out of the compartment beneath the radio. Satisfaction short-lived, Patrick tucked in his spent dick and returned to his slump behind the limo's wheel, aware of the digital clock's numbers as they tolled the time.

The cock-knocker had paid him well to be available, on call, so Patrick knew he'd punched his ticket, end of argument. But not the end of the story—a mystery, one growing more intriguing by the hour. Through the half-open privacy screen, he'd seen the two men scurry in from their private jet, so he knew they were *somebodies*. Cock-knocker's last name was Deveno. The only Deveno that Patrick knew was a wild man with huge hair and black fingernails from the big hair band, Stage Fright. The dude with the deep pockets didn't look anything like that Deveno.

The other guy that came with him was a tall bastard, lean and muscular, the kind you didn't dare fuck with. By the way he hid his face beneath the bill of a baseball cap, Patrick figured he was famous. But he only caught a fleeting look at the dude before he was seated with his back to the privacy screen, and the two of them were talking in grunts and whispers, only fragments of their conversations audible.

"You think this is gonna work?" Tall-dude asked.

Cock-knocker answered, "Wait until you see him. He's the spitting image of you, Duke. And the fucker can sing."

Duke. The mention of the name triggered another fractured memory in Patrick's brain. But it wasn't until the third man approached, hours after he collected the duo at the airport, that the memory unfolded fully from his gray matter. The third dude was the spitting image of Duke Dalton, who'd yanked his crank in front of a packed house at a concert somewhere in the Southwest. Like millions of curious net surfers, he'd found the video on YourTube. Most of the ones posted were shaky and didn't show all that much. One three-minute front row clip shot on a decent camera phone, however, captured Duke Dalton's sideshow act in stark detail, down to the hair on the big, painted-white balls hanging low beneath the hem of his lifted kilt.

Patrick had pumped off twice to that video, which was still listed under "Favorites" on his tablet.

Duke Dalton. That was the dude in the baseball cap! Had to be. So who was the third guy, who looked so much like him that they could have been twins? They'd picked him up at the Casino Club. Was he a musician, too? Then he remembered the snippet of conversation he'd heard through the open window. After jerking off and dumping the DNA-soaked napkin out the window, it struck him that regardless of the outcome, there was a story here.

And a profit to be made.

At three, Patrick pocketed his cell phone and left his post, locking up the limo behind him. He strutted through the garage, which sat dank and musty beneath the sallow, yellow lights. He crossed the pedestrian bridge to the hotel's lobby, catching his reflection in the acre of glass windows. As tall as Duke Dalton, lean, too, his was the body of an athlete. The black and white limo driver's uniform looked great on him. He wore a crisp white button-down shirt and thin black tie, black dress pants, socks, and shoes. Even the black leather fingerless gloves on his hands and chauffer's cap added a layer of sexy to his image. His nuts itched. Patrick scratched them on his march to the front desk.

"Can I help you?"

The dude behind the counter sounded as tired as Patrick felt. He was attractive but, Patrick thought, snorting a laugh, at three in the morning everyone was. A handsome dude with dark hair, a trim soul patch beneath his pouty lower lip, Latino, Patrick guessed, dressed in a hotel monkey suit. Another poor sucker like him, forced to labor through the late hours while the people with the money either slept or fucked.

Patrick gave the concierge a chin-tip in response. "Yeah, buddy, you got Internet access in here?"

The concierge—his name was Joaquin, according to the bronze tag on his lapel—said they did, only it was for guests.

"I'm a guest, sort of," Patrick said. He rattled off the room number of the luxury suite where Duke Dalton, his twin, and cock-knocker Deveno were likely passed out or playing with one another. "They stuck me down in the limo and I don't have my tablet on me. Dude, just for a sec, I swear. In and out."

"In and out," Joaquin repeated, licking at his lips.

At three in the morning, everything sounded dirty, and everyone awake was horny.

Patrick's dick tingled. Masturbating in the limo hadn't satisfied his needs, but he sensed that was about to change. "Thanks, *Joaquin*," he said, leaning over the desk and flashing his best seductive smile. "I really appreciate it."

"Why don't you come back here," Joaquin said, indicating the staff-only office behind the counter.

Patrick strutted over, aware of the flouncing weight of his cock. He gave it a shake for effect when he caught the concierge looking. At three in the morning, there are no drinks and very little discussion to lay the ground rules. Patrick knew Joaquin wanted to suck his dick, and Patrick planned to let him.

The office hummed with an undercurrent of electrical devices—computers and printers, a flat-screen TV running on low volume, and a row of security monitors. Joaquin was, apparently, the only actual body on duty in this section of the hotel. Patrick's tired mind locked on the notion of how easy it would be to rob the place. The only plunder he planned involved Joaquin's throat.

"There," the concierge said, indicating a desk with an enormous chair and a state-of-the-art desktop system. "Help yourself."

Joaquin then flashed a cocky smirk and felt up the front of Patrick's pants.

"There, help *yourself*, dude," Patrick fired back.

He took a seat in front of the computer. From the corner of his eye, he watched Joaquin hesitate, heard him take a dry and nervous swallow. Patrick knew he'd have to help the guy along.

Before logging into his email, he unzipped his pants. "Go to town, man."

Joaquin sank to his knees on the floor. For the next tense few seconds, while Patrick typed in his password, the other man worked his dick free from his underwear. Patrick's balls followed, and the musky scent of sweat mixed with the dregs of his recent nut drifted up, potent and exciting. Patrick waited. One of his balls vanished into the wet warmth of Joaquin's mouth.

"Aw, fuck yeah."

Eyes half-shut, Patrick drank in a deep breath, savoring the tug of Joaquin's throat on his nuts. The same killer sensation worked over his dick. Patrick growled a rosary of expletives. This was just what he needed. This, and the chance to make a decent score.

There it was, on the screen, his latest bank statement. Borderline anemic, tonight's job with the limo company would help, but he, like so many other dudes he knew, was living paycheck to paycheck, one emergency away from collapse. That sealed it.

Joaquin gave his balls a firm yank, bringing Patrick back to the moment. Wet, sucking heat engulfed his cock, making it difficult to think, to plan. Who was the dude who dogged rock bands, always trying to snap photos of them doing ridiculous shit, like hanging out on the beach with a nut or the heads of their dicks spilling out? The dude who'd gotten photos of Timberlake and Lachey in various stages of undress, the latter totally in the buff while sunbathing in a rented villa in Europe? Patrick only knew of the photographer because he liked to look, too.

He found the photos in his email after doing a search using Timberlake's name. The first that popped up was a candid photo of Jon Mayer, another of the rock-stalker's favorite subjects. Marquis Stilton, that was the guy.

"You're fucking hot, man," Joaquin moaned, his hot breath raining over Patrick's balls.

Patrick felt a rush of fresh sweat break out along his hairline, growing beneath his chauffer's cap. But the building deluge had less to do with Joaquin's expert oral skills than the certainty that Marquis Stilton would pay him decently for this kind of information, and pay him well.

Following the link to the photographer's official site took extra effort. At three in the morning, the skill with which Joaquin worked his tool was nothing less than that of an expert. Not only Patrick's cock but also his entire body seemed part of the experience, his throat, toes, earlobes, and nipples feeling hewn of the same erectile tissue. Patrick's balls swung low in the loose skin of his sac. Were they always that big? Big fucking come-tanks, full of juice. So much juice that it was bubbling up, painting Joaquin's tongue, the excess giving him a milk mustache whenever he strummed Patrick's dick with his lips.

Focus, dude, he told himself. Patrick fondled his balls. Joaquin sucked harder, taking his dick down to the pelt. Focusing wouldn't be the easiest thing to accomplish, but he had to try. Patrick released his balls and scrolled through the menu. Marquis Stilton didn't post his phone number—sleazy, yes, but no dummy. There was, however, an email address. Patrick clicked it on. Up popped the e-mail box.

One of the truths about being mostly awake and alert at three in the morning is that some things, like sex, come easier. And some basic activities are more difficult.

Patrick typed into the body of the e-mail three times and erased the lines an equal number because the words he put down were a jumble of nonsense. Finally, he wrote that he had an interesting scoop on the lead singer of 3-D, Duke Dalton, and that Stilton should contact him on his cell if he was interested in learning more. Patrick typed his phone number. Simple, to the point. He hit send and reclined in the chair. A few seconds later, he nutted.

"Thanks, amigo," Patrick sighed.

Swallowing, Joaquin said, "Thank you, man," licked his lips, and then cleaned up the dregs of Patrick's climax, lapping at the flow from his slit.

"You're welcome."

Joaquin adjusted the lump in his pants. "Wish I had more time, but I need to get back out there."

Good, thought Patrick. He might have given the concierge a tug—Joaquin was cute—but now that he'd busted his load, Patrick's interest in more than a blowjob had cooled considerably.

"You all done in here?"

"Yeah, I appreciate it," Patrick said. He clicked out of his e-mail and stood, shook off his cock, tucked it back in, and zipped.

"What's your name?" Joaquin asked.

"Simon," Patrick lied, not sure why.

Patrick checked his cell, making sure it was on, and exited the office. His balls felt drained and tight now. Casting a sideways glance at Joaquin, he imagined the handsome fucker's belly was full of his skeet, an early breakfast of pure protein. Patrick smirked. He'd come, seen, and conquered, for sure.

He was halfway across the pedestrian bridge when his phone chirped. A squirt of adrenaline jolted Patrick out of his happy stupor. At first, he worried that it was the Deveno dude, the cock-knocker. He saw that the caller's number was listed as private. Deveno had given Patrick his cell number in case of any trouble.

He stabbed the answer button. "Yo."

"Yo yourself," a snippy voice that sounded like a mouth full of marbles answered. "You just e-mailed me."

"Is this Marquis?"

"It is."

"My man, I'm Patrick. Dude… I love your work. That photo you posted of the Red Hot Chili—"

"Fuck the Peppers, man. You said you had something for me on 3-D and Duke Dalton."

Patrick sucked in a deep hit of breath, held it, and then just as deeply let it out in an attempt to still his pulse. "Oh, yeah. I fucking do, man."

"I'm listening."

"First, you'd better be transferring. *Money*, that is, 'cause I'm not giving this away for free."

A humorless chuckle filtered over the line. "How do I know you're legit, or that the information you're trying to bilk me for is even worth it?"

"I guess you don't," Patrick said. Coolness cascaded down his spine, surprisingly chilly in the bottled warmth inside the pedestrian bridge that connected hotel to garage. "But that's the risk you're gonna have to run, dude, because if you don't buy it, someone else will. And I'd rather work with you—as I've already said, you're *the man*. I ain't just buttering your balls."

Another chuckle, this one wasn't so stale. "And I do love having my balls buttered. Okay, here's the deal. You show me something that proves you're not a crackpot with useless information and I'll wire you my standard rate."

"Which is?"

Marquis rattled off a number. Patrick's nuts pulled out of their tightness and his cock began to swell.

"Fucking-A," Patrick sighed.

"Duke Dalton's been off the radar since he beat his meat in Austin. What I wouldn't give to find out what's been happening in his sweaty shorts since."

Patrick smiled. "I can tell you, dude. I'm driving his fucking limo."

"Get me a photo to prove it, with a date and time stamp. E-mail it to me and we'll talk."

Patrick said he would—no problem. "Great to be working with you, man."

"That has yet to be seen. I'll be in touch," the voice at the other end of the connection said before hanging up.

Patrick pocketed the phone and continued the rest of the way to the limo, his half-hard dick swinging in his pants, dollar signs in his eyes.

The opportunity came as the three men were piling into the back of the limo. In lieu of sleeping, Patrick had spent the early morning rehearsing the method, angling the camera in his phone so that it captured the image perfectly. Ignoring his nerves, he clicked the photo, sure the cock-knocker would pitch a fit. He didn't. Patrick checked the capture. There they were, Deveno and two dudes. The one they'd picked up at the Casino Club was dressed in a tracksuit. Duke Dalton, he was sure, now wore the third guy's clothes—shirt, jeans, even his sneakers.

Patrick studied them through the open partition on the long drive back to the Casino Club, taking mental notes. He was ready to receive an influx of cash and wanted to be armed with as many of the facts as possible.

They dropped Duke in front of the third dude's shitty car. Right after pulling away, headed to the airport, Deveno cranked the privacy screen, and Patrick swore the adorable little fuck with the goatee and the stud that looked a hell of a lot like Duke Dalton were going at it. His cock remained stiff the rest of the way there, though he couldn't be sure if it was because the two dudes were fucking around, making the limo bounce as it motored down the highway, or the promise of the score they'd unwittingly tossed in his lap.

"Okay, I believe you," said Marquis Stilton. "That's a hell of a photo. Makes me want to know more."

"I know more. A lot more."

"I've made the transfer into your checking account, for services rendered. As soon as the wire clears, I'll expect you to call... and to render services. Here's the number."

Patrick jotted it down.

"Now that we're old buddies, I'm looking forward to working with you," Marquise said.

Patrick smiled and groped his dick. "Word."

Track 7

DUKE SEIZED IN place behind the wheel. The man standing outside leaned down. He was attractive beyond cute, with eyes that blended into the palette of grays and a look of confusion once those moody blues connected with his emerald greens.

"Seamus?" the man asked, his voice muffled behind the window glass.

Duke choked down a dry smile. "Hey, man."

The guy narrowed his eyes. "What's going on?"

What was going on, Duke sensed, was that Seamus and the body standing on the other side of the door shared history. Recent history, probably, but there was a link, something electric and chemical. Dare he think it? Seamus and this dude had fucked around, if the undercurrent rippling through the overcast was to be trusted.

He started to panic. What the hell had he expected—to not run into anybody Seamus Whyler knew while on his vision quest? Duke rolled down the window. A gust of humid air poured in along with the man's clean scent, soap and skin, basic yet intoxicating.

"Just... on my way to, you know, play," Duke said, aiming a thumb at the guitar resting on the piles of things in the back seat.

"I told you that you could stay with me while you're in town, at my place," the man said. Then, his voice dropping almost to a whisper, he added, "You know how much I love it when you play."

There it was, the proof. Seamus and the attractive man had gotten horizontal. A picture flashed through Duke's mind, of the guy on his knees, his mouth wrapped around Seamus's uncircumcised dick; those lips, mere inches from his now, had licked his reflection's balls, tasted his seed, perhaps eaten his ass. The urge to kiss the dude nearly overwhelmed Duke. Only the pressure of the unease creeping in through the window stopped him.

"Who the fuck are you?" the young man demanded.

"It's me, Seamus. Seamus Whyler," Duke lied.

"You look like him, but I sure as hell know the difference—you're not him."

Duke choked down a dry swallow. "But I am."

"If you're Seamus, what's my name?"

Duke reached for the keys in the ignition. The car grumbled to life. "It's not what you think."

A fist hammered the window. "Don't you dare drive away, not until you tell me where Seamus is. The *real* Seamus."

Duke threw the car in reverse. The guy jumped out of the way. Only after he was speeding up the coast did he realize he'd nearly run over the other man's toes in his haste to escape.

Escape.

Muggy, salty air streamed into the car, stirring the senses, stoking his boldness. He had escaped the life of Duke Dalton and his alter ego, Duke De Morte, and he'd gotten past the one and only gatekeeper between he and Seamus Whyler's borrowed identity. He *was* Seamus Whyler.

Duke roared, "*Yee-haw!*" out the window and drove on. The rain fell, thinly at first, but in ever-increasing density, the sheets, like his shower, washing away his sins.

He glanced in the rearview mirror and saw the guitar. Duke took the next exit and followed it past the gas stations and fast food restaurants until he came upon salt marsh flats briny with the stink of swamps mixed with saline. He parked the car. The rain let up some twenty minutes later. Duke stepped out. A gray patch of Atlantic loomed beyond the cattails and tall marsh grasses. The sun broke partially free of the clouds, a platinum disk hovering behind a veil of ashes.

He moved with confidence toward the back door, but on the inside, Duke was all raw nerve. A flock of agitated yellow jackets had taken up residence inside his stomach and were swarming angrily at being jostled. Duke opened the rear right door and pulled out the guitar. No magical spark of golden light erupted at the contact or stilled the wasps inside him. If anything, their stingers dug deeper into the soft lining of his guts.

It was your basic acoustic model, neck and strings and wood. But as he hefted it from one hand to another and plucked, finding it perfectly tuned, something did happen. Hope replaced his fear.

Duke climbed onto the wet hood of the car and assumed a casual pose, legs kicked over the edge, one foot planted on the front bumper. He plucked and fucked around for a few minutes, staring at the platinum sun and the gray wedge of ocean. This was, he imagined, like watching the very first day in the history of the world and, in a way, it was. His first morning free of the burdens associated with being Duke Dalton.

Music... it had always been a huge part of his life, one of those constants hardwired into him like eating or breathing. Looking back, he couldn't think of a time when he hadn't been playing an instrument or crooning a tune. Somewhere in the old man's house were tapes that he'd made of Duke singing, some as far back as diapers, so the story went.

He and Harley had been part of a select group, tutored on the road or at an exclusive school for the gifted when they weren't traveling with the band. Most people didn't appreciate the significance of food when their stomachs were full, any more than they thought about air until they were suffocating. Music was like that to him. Always there. Involuntary.

Only now on the hood of another man's car it wasn't. Duke stopped playing, closed his eyes, and felt the constant flow vanish, depleted or driven out, he couldn't tell which. He started to suffocate and then realized he was holding his breath. Duke's stomach rumbled; room service breakfast at the Wilver Court Hotel in Boston felt days behind him now. He was hungry, out of breath, and absent of music. A blank slate, starting over from scratch.

Duke sucked in another greedy sip of breath and raised the guitar. His fingers twitched, desperate to play, but he stilled them for a moment.

"What's the first song that you remember totally obsessing over?" he asked aloud.

The wind rose in a gentle whisper, as though answering. The smell of the ocean reached him, invigorating in its newness. Without prompting, his fingers began to strum, and the music, though basic, was perfect.

"*Bien chéveré,*" he said, mumbling lyrics, speaking words. The words and the chords merged seamlessly.

He gave an acoustic performance of Stevie Wonder's "Don't You Worry 'Bout a Thing" to no one but the seagulls and sand crabs, which was eerily fitting considering he was in a strange town, driving a strange car that was not only vehicle but his only shelter, with a pittance in his wallet. He was cut off from everyone and everything familiar, but strange as it all was, it was also wonderful. His voice carried across the marsh.

"Don't you worry 'bout a thing," he sang in perfect pitch. By the end of the song, Duke believed the lyrics.

After several hours playing a greatest hits collection of his favorite songs, everything from Olivia Newton-John ballads to Anthrax screamers, the rain resumed and hunger got the better of him, so Duke drove in search of sustenance, backtracking down the coast to Bay Breeze.

The downpour drove away all but the most hardcore beachgoers and the surfer dudes from the beach. Duke found a little burger and seafood shack, pocketed his keys, and hurried through the rain into the casual and colorful restaurant.

The waitress seated him at the bar at his request. Flying solo without an entourage for the first time in... *forever*, he realized... was disorienting. The bar seemed a fitting spot for a lone wolf musician.

"Musician," he repeated, loving the sound of it. Not *rock star*, but *musician*, which conjured a happy little grin. Like being alone, for the first time, Duke felt like a real music maker.

The waitress presented him with a menu and rattled off the day's specials, most of which were fresh, locally caught seafood with a price tag he wouldn't have balked at under normal circumstances. Duke never checked costs, and he loved seafood. He was about to order the fisherman's platter, knowing it would taste heavenly, when he remembered that his wallet stuffed with cash and unlimited credit on numerous cards was soaring over the Rockies, warmed against Seamus Whyler's butt. He had Seamus's, and there wasn't a lot of the green stuff in it.

He settled for a burger instead, with fries, water, wedge of lemon instead of soda. Duke shook salt on his fries and doused them with ketchup and, to his satisfaction, it turned out being the best meal he could recall enjoying as he cleaned his plate.

Duke peeled off his shoes and socks and walked down to the water, the guitar strapped to his back. The sand beneath his toes launched electric pinpricks up his legs. He waded in to his knees, the icy rush almost as invigorating as enjoying the day's meal, the day's music.

The gentle crash of waves at low tide permeated the dark afternoon. An early twilight was due to arrive, owing to the overcast. Duke walked back to the beach, sat on the cement ledge at the breakwater, and played his guitar. Another of those old songs from his youth sprang forth, without preparation or fanfare. Gilbert O'Sullivan's "Alone Again, Naturally."

He was so entranced in the lyrics, the melody, Duke didn't realize a small crowd had gathered comprised of two hot babes, surfers in their wetsuits, and an older gentleman. The older guy sucked on an obscenely long cigar. When Duke concluded the song, ending it on a throaty high note that would have made O'Sullivan proud, the crowd broke in applause.

"Hey, that was you last night in the Casino Club, right?" the fogie with the stogie asked.

"You were great," the hot blonde holding onto his arm added.

Duke smiled. "Thanks."

"Where's your guitar case?" the fogie asked, pulling out his wallet. He fished a twenty from inside and handed it over.

Duke smiled and accepted the money. "Seriously, man, thank you."

He thought about what to play next. Something by the Eagles, maybe. He strummed a few chords. The audience of less than a dozen listened intently. Duke faced the fogie, who puffed away on his cigar, hands tucked in his pockets. "Can you do me a favor?"

"Depends," the man said around his cigar.

"You got a book of matches on you?"

"You smoke?" the fogie asked.

"No, I just like to save a little something from everywhere I play. A souvenir."

He belted out "Hotel California" and followed it with a slow, smoky rendition of the old Johnny Mathis tune, "When Sunny Gets Blue." When he wasn't warping young minds and screaming such memorable rock standards as "Chest of Death" and "Girl with the Golden Tongue," Duke's dad, Jack Dalton, had loved to play Johnny Mathis in the house.

Duke's pulse raced. He pulled out the twenty he'd earned on the beach and handed it to the man in the ticket booth who eyed him curiously.

"Didn't you play here last night?"

"That's me," Duke said. "Seamus Whyler."

"Thought so. Your money's no good here tonight—just go on in, man."

Duke took the ticket and the twenty bucks and thanked the man. The twenty felt like a million in his pocket.

The Casino Club was a shadowy expanse of white tables for two or four, spread in an oblong pattern around a center stage. There, a trio performed classic Brubeck—saxophonist, pianist, and guitarist. The haunting, happy chords of "Take Five" spread across the club, counterpointed by conversations and the clink of wine glasses.

A waitress glided over to take his drink order. Duke asked for a soda with a wedge of lemon. The man who'd stood outside the car window earlier demanding to know what he'd done with the real Seamus Whyler delivered the drink.

"Give me one reason why I shouldn't call the cops," the man said between a trilling saxophone.

Duke studied the dude's face in the grayness. Damn cute. "Because no crime's been committed."

"Where's Seamus?"

"Probably eating a hundred-dollar steak while getting his feet massaged."

The cute-face folded his arms and snorted. "What?"

Duke leaned closer. "Look, this isn't anything sinister. I'm simply switching places with Seamus for a while. Giving him a taste of the luxury lifestyle while filling in for him. It's perfectly legit."

"I don't get it," the face said.

Duke wondered of that statement's dual edges—the not understanding and the not-getting sex with Seamus. He could easily fix one of the statement's turns. Both, now that he thought about it.

Leaning closer, Duke said, "I think Seamus is a very lucky man to have you looking after his well-being and needs."

The man's stony expression softened some. "I'm lucky to have him to look after when he's in town. But you still haven't explained this switcheroo. Who the fuck are you?"

"Would you have a drink with me? Give me a chance to explain?"

The face waved the waitress over and ordered another soda. When it arrived, he held his up. Duke raised his glass. They toasted.

"To Seamus," the face said. "Now, out with the truth—or you're going to wear this drink, dude."

His name was Toby Cosgrove and he was the club's events coordinator, the guy who booked acts. The dude who routinely gave Seamus a venue to play.

"Wow," Duke said.

"What do you mean by 'wow'?"

Duke glanced around. He'd never played a club this small before. *Intimate* was the better word, he mentally corrected. Every time 3-D had taken to the stage it was an event. But something had been lost in not knowing the audience in such close quarters. Duke didn't know if he could explain that to Toby Cosgrove. He also wasn't sure he'd make it out of the club alive if he didn't come clean. Toby's gaze drilled into him.

"I'm going out on a limb here and trusting you with this, man. My name is Duke Dalton. I'm the lead singer of the band—"

"3-D?" Toby interjected. "The guy who basted his batter all over the front row in Dallas?"

"It was in Austin, actually, but yeah, that's me. I'd say the one and only, only it turns out that old saying about us all having a double somewhere in the world is true. Mine's Seamus Whyler. Last night, you spoke to my assistant."

"The guy with the goatee?"

Duke nodded. "For months, I've had him on the lookout to find a talented singer who could pass for me on stage while I take a breather, get some air, some distance."

Toby's narrowed eyes scanned him. "Holy shit. So you hired Seamus to...?"

"To be me until I figure out what the fuck it all means."

The skeptical mask Toby had worn from the moment they met cracked. "Duke De Morte? I have two of your CDs."

Duke extended his big hand across the table. "A pleasure to meet you, man."

Toby's throat knotted with a noticeable swallow. He reached across the table, his smaller hand vanishing into Duke's. The two men shook. The fit, Duke thought, was strangely familiar, as comfortable as Seamus Whyler's old shoes and unremarkable guitar.

"So," he sighed, in no particular hurry to break the shake. "You and Seamus, you're friends?"

Toby fixed him with a stare. "Friends, sure."

"Friends with benefits?"

Their hands remained locked. An hour and a half after that, they staggered into Toby's beachfront cottage, mouths locked together. Toby's fingers sought the bulge in Duke's jeans. Duke grabbed the other man's ass, eager to enjoy it once he freed it from its prison of blue jeans.

"I told Seamus he could crash here," Toby said between kisses. "That if he needed a place, he had one."

"Does that offer apply to me?"

"It does for tonight."

Duke smiled and pulled Toby into a bear hug.

Track 8

SEAMUS JOLTED AWAKE, gasping for breath that refused to come easily. The nightmare lingered, exerting its pull in layers of invisible ice that clung to his flesh. Panicking, he didn't recognize the vast strokes of red staining the walls like bloody gashes or the phantoms of unfamiliar furniture. The only furniture he once owned was back at Wanda's house.

He was in a bed. Seamus rarely slept in beds; he was a sofa-surfing kind of guy, a dude who passed out behind the wheel of his car more often than not. Then his racing mind remembered he wasn't Seamus Whyler anymore.

His surroundings stabilized and Seamus recognized the furniture and bold red artwork. They were Duke Dalton's. The artwork, Harley had explained, was one of a kind, original. Museum-quality, by a famous modern painter. To Seamus, they looked like somebody had dipped their brush in a gallon of ruby-red and covered two oblong canvases, which anyone could do. Only not just anyone had, Harley had reminded him. The price tag on the pair was in the high-five figures. Seamus had nearly passed out as the absurdity registered. What he could do with that kind of money! Paint a few thousand canvases in red, for instance.

The bed was comfortable—too comfortable—and he didn't care for it. Glancing at the clock, Seamus saw that it was a little after midnight, an hour after he'd gone down following the house tour. He reached between his legs to play with his balls and found them huddled against the root of his cock for warmth, his sac tightened into leather.

In the nightmare, he was on stage with 3-D, dressed in the sharp black and white suit ensemble that would decay the instant the black light zeroed in on him. Suddenly, he couldn't play the guitar. No sounds emerged as his hands, which had become blocks of stone, strummed over the strings. When he'd opened his mouth to sing, he was mute, with the whole world watching.

Seamus pulled into a fetal curl beneath the bedspread. Gradually, his heartbeat stilled and he got his breathing under control. The chill laying over his skin evaporated and his balls loosened after the truth about the dream hit home fully. Jitters about performing with the band, that was all. *Good old stage fright*, he thought, aware of the irony. It didn't help that he hadn't touched his guitar in well over a day. Twenty-four very long hours, and then some. The longest he'd gone without playing or singing since that day beside the stone wall and his father's angry fists.

From the time he'd gotten on Duke's private jet, music had been the farthest thing from his new itinerary.

The 3-D private jet landed smoothly. The flight had been extremely comfortable. With Seamus's dick sated after the expert hummer Harley provided in the back of the limo, his stomach's needs were attended to with tuna wasabi rolls, leafy salad, and cold summer fruit. He had his choice of a dozen new-release in-flight movies. Seamus hadn't seen a movie in months. He settled back, put up his feet, and drank designer water, loving this small preview of his rock star's life.

Another car picked them up at the airport and shuttled them through the Hollywood Hills to Dymond Encerito, a famous Beverly Hills landmark situated behind a gated drive and presently Duke Dalton's private estate. The compound boasted a main house and guest cottage, a recording studio, pool, and towering palms. Orange and blue flowers that looked like living origami swayed in dense gardens leading up to the front door. Birds-of-paradise, Harley said, catching his study of the exotic blossoms.

The house was a man's sort of place, beige and without much thought. Duke Dalton's bedroom, one of eight in the manor, had the master's masculine stamp in dark wood furniture, a bedspread the color of denim, and those ridiculous red paintings. Everything boasted an ordered look, including the closets filled with clothes and shoes, many of the latter still in their shoeboxes, as yet unworn.

Nothing in the main house suggested a famous rock star lived there. Granted, the man cave—which was about as big as Carlsbad Cavern in New Mexico—was outfitted with every bonus imaginable: theater sound system, giant flat-screen TV, the latest video games, and a classic Wurlitzer jukebox. But the rock posters, platinum records, and mementos that Seamus expected to see instead of overpriced kid's art were missing.

"I stay in the room down there," Harley said, indicating one of the three downstairs bedrooms. "My office is right next door."

"Convenient," Seamus said.

The first-floor kitchen was huge, with Carrera marble countertops and an eight-burner gourmet stove that sparkled, seeming to indicate that the band ate out a lot. Across from the kitchen and formal dining room was an understated den with overstuffed sofas, a TV, and a view of the pool and recording studio, which was housed in a one-story, sound-insulated bungalow.

After tossing and turning for another half hour in Duke Dalton's too-comfortable bed, Seamus threw back the covers and stood. Most of the life had returned to his balls, which had descended out of their huddle and were enjoying plenty of low hang. His cock swung over them, calling out to his hand for attention. The designer briefs Duke had presented to him earlier lay discarded at the side of the bed, along with his socks. Seamus grabbed a pillow and the comforter and walked out of the room, tromping down the stairs to the den.

The sofas were like fabric marshmallows. Seamus tossed his pillow and then his ass onto the largest of the three. Now this was a bed!

Before sleep claimed him, Seamus's eyes drifted toward the line of windows with their view of the pool and the recording studio. The skies in New Hampshire had been a mess of rain clouds. Here, they were clear and a chunk of not-quite-full moon rained light across the compound. The pool glowed. The recording studio shimmered out of focus beyond, an apparition beckoning to him.

That little bungalow, deceptively small on the outside, was a musician's dream. Comfortable, overstuffed furniture like the sofa beneath his spine populated an informal sitting area whose walls were covered with the framed posters and platinum records missing from the main house. Vinyl records, cassette tapes, and CDs filled shelves and racks. Priceless rock memorabilia in acrylic boxes and frames, like Ringo's *Sergeant Pepper* costume and an authentic Devo lid hat from the 1980 "Whip It" video added to the décor. There were framed photos on one wall, each showing Duke shaking hands with a Who's Who of the famous and infamous, the ingenious and insane, most still living and making music, some now singing for the angels. And that was just the great room.

A fully insulated recording studio sat behind floor-to-ceiling glass that Seamus guessed was thick enough to stop bullets. The instruments on the stage area were top of the line. According to Harley, so were the ones in the sound booth.

Standing in there, Seamus had wondered how any man with music in his heart could claim to be numb and disconnected. He'd grabbed the nearest Fender off its stand and was poised to go to town when Harley held up a hand.

"The guys will be here first thing in the morning. Why don't we eat, rest."

Seamus scratched his balls. Some rest—a half dozen steps into the main house, Harley dropped to his knees. They ate, all right.

In the silence and moonlight, Seamus resisted the urge to sleep. He ordered his big feet off the sofa, to march out there, naked as he was, and into the studio. There, he planned to write down the lines of a new song that had tormented him since he boarded the private jet. Pick up a guitar, he would. Crank some tunes. Get lost in the wonderland just beyond the pool.

"Fuck," Seamus sighed.

But he couldn't because, as Harley had reminded him, he was no longer a solo act. He was part of a band now, and he would have to adopt a different mindset. Was it any wonder Duke was having trouble feeling the magic?

As he lies there, drifting to a state not quite sleep, Seamus wondered if his new freedom wasn't really just a different kind of prison, one with golden bars.

THE RAIN BROKE, along with the humidity. The air whispering into the cottage was dry and smelled of the sea except nearest the bed, where the musty odor of sex lingered, reminding Duke of the previous night's fun whenever the breeze lifted.

Duke rolled over. The adorable face on the other pillow was already studying him through sleepy eyes above lips surrounded by morning stubble that was unfairly sexy.

"Morning," Toby said. "Or should I say, morning *wood*."

A hand under the top sheet gripped Duke's dick. He growled, "Yup, wood it is."

Toby leaned closer. Their lips met. Duke tasted the bitter tang of the last load he'd dumped via their kiss.

The cadence of waves hitting the shore serenaded in the background. A rush of excitement pulsed through his blood, having little to do with the fondling of his cock. The emotion was almost giddy in its power, foreign in its nature. Only after Toby broke their lip lock did Duke identify it as happiness. He'd woken beside a body he wanted to be with in a cottage on the beach, to a day filled with possibilities.

He stretched out on the bed and spread his legs, surprised that his cock was up and ready after coming twice in the other man's mouth. The first had happened quickly. The second nut had taken longer, delivered without haste to the soundtrack of the storm rattling the house and the crash of the waves. This third time, he noted with a smile, would be bathed in morning sunlight.

Toby's kisses reached the tangle of curls lining Duke's pubis. A few licks over Duke's balls followed, and then a warm mouth engulfed his cock.

"Oh, fuck," Duke moaned. "Dude, you're amazing."

Toby spit him out and said, "Thanks, you too."

Their gazes met, and that icy-hot flicker teasing his insides surged back. It wasn't love—it couldn't be, not this quickly. That kind of love simply didn't exist outside of saccharine ballads. Then again, how did he know that for sure? Yeah, he cared for Harley, though that was a friendly sort of affection. This felt different.

Toby's mouth plunged down again and Duke panicked. He didn't want it to end, but his ass was on the move, extricating his dick from Toby's face, before he could rationalize his sudden maneuvers.

"Dude, you okay?"

"Yes, just a little sore," Duke lied. A nervous smile crossed his face. "You mind if I take a walk? I'm feeling the need to stretch my legs."

The disappointment on Toby's face was obvious. "Fine," he said, and Duke sensed that, too, was a lie. Toby settled back against the pillows, hawked some spit on his hand, and started masturbating. For one blinding instant, all Duke could think about was diving between the cheeks of the man's ass and eating him all the way to climax. Only he'd made his move, and the confusion was growing instead of siphoning off.

Duke grabbed his shirt, underwear, and jeans, leaving shoes and socks in the pile where they'd fallen during the night's rabid fumbling.

"Will you be here when I get back?" Duke asked at the bedroom door, stuffing his cock undercover.

"Sure will," Toby said. He continued to stroke his erection openly, without shame. Not that the dude had any reason to feel guilt or be embarrassed.

Next to the music Duke so desperately longed to connect with, meeting Toby Cosgrove was the biggest blessing of this new life.

He walked along the shore, savoring the feel of the sugary grains beneath his toes and the way the sunshine dappled on the water. On this bright morning, the beach was considerably more populated. Smartly, he'd grabbed Seamus's old baseball cap from the car. Better to be safe than risk recognition by some zealous fan.

Toby... *fuck*, Duke cursed in silence. What was he thinking by walking away, right as the dude was showing his dick such righteous love? Love, that was the problem. He was a little too old for crushes, but probably far too young to be this pessimistic. *Maybe he'd enjoyed way too much sex*, he thought with a humorless chuckle. Sex had always been available, and it was conceivable that it had eclipsed his ability to recognize the possibility of something more than a nut-and-run situation.

He didn't know if he loved Toby, but Duke sure did *like* the guy, and wasn't that just as important?

A lightness came over him, and he started to turn around. If he hurried back, he'd likely be there in time to stick his tongue up Toby's ass, or shepherd him with a tug to the balls, an extra hand around his dick. They'd kiss and, perhaps, the interrupted blowjob would resume.

Only he didn't realize how far he'd already traveled. Bay Breeze spread before him, a little seaside town with an amusement park and tourist traps and stands that sold fried dough and wafer-thin pizza by the slice. Duke had been on plenty of beaches before, some of the planet's best—San Trope, Cannes, Miami—but never this alone, this focused.

A beach tune formed in his thoughts, something very classic. It took humming the tune for him to realize that it was "A Summer Place." He followed it up with an appropriate a capella number by The Beach Boys, only it sounded like Van Halen's remake halfway through. A little

Enya, sailing away, and then the opening of the movie *Grease*, on the beach, with Sandy Olsen and Danny Zuko frolicking to the melody of "Love is a Many Splendored Thing."

Of course he was feeling inspired, thanks to the sun's light raining down and the smell of the sea and suntan lotion and the sand beneath his toes unleashing smaller versions of an orgasm with every step. He didn't know what he wanted to grab hold of first when he entered the house—Toby or the guitar. Maybe he'd reach for both.

The little cottage appeared at long last, a charming square of weathered boards beneath a peaked metal roof, wedged between two other tiny houses, all similar in shape, no doubt constructed by the same builder decades ago. Duke bounded up the three steps to the screened door and into the front room, which was a combination kitchen, dining room, and living room.

Toby appeared at the bedroom door, dressed in blue jeans and a fresh T-shirt. The scent of soap that carried around him and the image of his bare feet at the bottom of his blue jeans drained the moisture from Duke's mouth while sending all of his blood into his dick. It would be Toby and then the guitar, in that order.

"Hey," Duke said.

"Hey yourself."

Duke moved closer, tucking his hands into his pockets. His fingers brushed his cock, and he almost gasped at the unexpected jolt of pleasure.

"So?" Toby ventured.

"So, *this*." Duke bridged the distance and pulled the other man into his arms. A rush of smells teased Duke's senses, not only the soap but also Toby's shampoo, a basic and masculine brand, and the salt air.

Their lips crushed together. Duke worked his tongue into Toby's mouth. For a brief and wonderful time, that part of their anatomy wrestled. Toby tasted of mint toothpaste, which enhanced Duke's pleasure, though he missed the dregs of his maleness marking Toby as his own, which the shower had washed away.

Duke seized one of Toby's hands and guided it toward his swell. Toby obliged him with a squeeze, only to withdraw his touch. Their tongues untwined, and lips parted.

"What is it?" Duke asked.

A smile broke on Toby's lips, but the gesture looked pained instead of happy. "Like you said, you're not Seamus."

"No, I'm not."

"I won't say I'm in love with the dude, but I like him. A lot."

"I appreciate that. I get it."

"Do you?"

Toby leaned his head on Duke's shoulder. Duke caught another hit of shampoo and, for a blinding instant, all he could think about was how badly he wanted them to fuck.

"Seamus is a hell of a guy," Duke said, unsure of what else to or where the conversation was headed.

"I know how broke he is, which is why I try to book him as often as possible. My way of looking out for him, doing what I can, even though I sometimes catch hell from my boss."

Duke reached up and ran his fingers through Toby's short athletic cut. "I bet Seamus really appreciates it."

"I went down on him the other night, for the first time."

Duke raised an eyebrow. "I bet he really appreciated *that*."

"Point is, I like the guy. I like you."

"Thanks," Duke said. "And right back at you."

"But…"

"But?"

Toby lifted his head and their eyes connected. "I'd be willing to consider the possibility of something more than just blowjobs."

"You want me to fuck you?"

Toby's gaze bore into him. "I'd prefer you to *date* me."

Track 9

THE SUNLIGHT STREAMING through the windows and a full bladder conspired to wake Seamus. He tossed aside the blanket and staggered away from the sofa, his morning hard-on tick-tocking proudly in front of him.

He navigated the way to the nearest of the downstairs bathrooms on memory, passing through the acre of kitchen and dining room. Halfway through, Seamus realized there were bodies in the kitchen, four of them. He ceased strutting and stroking his cock, stopping on a dime.

"Morning, dude," one of the four men enjoying coffee and talking in whispers said.

Seamus felt his face flush. He waved. "'Sup?"

"I'd say *you*," another of the men snickered.

The third stranger—Harley stood at the sink pouring coffee into a tall mug—was a fierce-looking fucker, stone-faced, with a military haircut and ink down one full arm and a leg. Had to be Joe-Kev Hallet, the band's badass drummer. Seamus sensed the man's roving eyes absorbing his nakedness from top to bottom.

"Uh, I should grab some pants," Seamus stammered.

"Don't bother. We're a fairly loose bunch," the first man said. He was tall and lanky, with an insanely attractive face that hadn't yet seen a razor on this morning. "The less clothes, the better. At least for me. I'm Shaye, 3-D's keyboardist."

"Dude," Seamus said. He reached his shake-hand over, realized he'd been using it to shake his erection, and then wiped it off on his hip before sending it back. "Love your work, especially the solo in 'Smashing Plates'—genius, truly."

"Aw, now you're just trying to get me to suck your dick," Shaye said, meeting his gesture.

The two men shook.

"While you're down there," Seamus joked.

"Fuck you, man."

Laughter filled the kitchen.

Harley handed over the big coffee cup. Seamus took it and sidled his bare ass onto one of the barstools. "Let's go through the rest of the introductions. Shaye, you've met... and apparently, had oral sex with. That's Arif, on bass, better known as—"

"Scalpel, yeah, I know."

"And the one who looks like he just ate a live puppy over there, that ugly son of a whore's Joe-Kev, also known as 'Autopsy'."

Seamus saluted, aware that Joe-Kev's gaze never left him. He wasn't even sure if the fucker blinked. Joe-Kev grunted something in response.

The coffee was strong and desperately needed.

"We didn't mean to wake you," Harley said. "We tried to be quiet."

"You didn't wake me. He did." Seamus gave his boner a playful backhand. "Listen, I'm happy to hang out like this... emphasis on the hanging. But first, I need to drain my vein and, next, I should probably at least put on some underwear."

Seamus eased off the barstool and continued down the hall, toward the closest head.

"I don't believe it," he heard Arif say over his shoulder. "He's the mirror image of Duke."

"Yeah, you see the hog on the dude?" This came from Shaye. "He's just like Duke, in every detail."

"There is one difference," said Harley.

Seamus dipped into the bathroom and toyed with his foreskin, gliding it back and forth, loving the way it made his entire body tingle.

He trotted down the stairs, dressed in loose-fit cotton shorts and a T-shirt he pulled from a stack that looked to be a hundred deep in one of the closets.

The band had relocated to the living room. From the moment Seamus entered, he could tell that the levity was gone. It was all business now.

"There's no need to restate the situation—we're all on the same page," Harley said. "From this point forward, Seamus will be Duke in every regard. I can tell you for a fact that the guy can sing, so we don't have anything to worry about there."

"That remains to be seen in the studio," said Arif. "Baptism by fire. Hope he can handle the heat."

Seamus finished his coffee in one gulp. "Watch me."

"We will," Shaye said. "So will everyone out there in the audience, along with their camera phones, and the media. Don't mean to bust those low-hanging balls of yours, man, but you know what you're in for, right?"

"Bring it on," he said, all cock-sure on the outside while silently, inwardly, Seamus expected that deep gulp of coffee to reappear at any second.

The day was your typical perfect Southern California beauty, dry and warm. The smell of citrus from the lemon and orange trees heavy with fruit growing around the compound couldn't have looked more perfect on the surface.

But Seamus sensed an undercurrent of energy building in the air, like the shift in barometric pressure that signals a violent spell of weather is on its way.

He hadn't experienced stage fright in some time, not since college and even that hadn't affected his performance. For the time it took to navigate around the pool, Seamus considered it possible he was feeling star struck. Then he dismissed that, too. 3-D was an amazing band with a unique style and he was stoked to be part of it. On the final approach to the studio, it dawned on him that the nerves clawing at his insides, making his adrenal gland squirt miserable fluids into his bloodstream, were on high alert because while Duke Dalton had signed off, this was, in effect, an audition with the rest of the band.

The most important audition of his career.

Before their first studio session, he changed into a pair of cargo shorts that hugged his ass wickedly, along with a couple of chains he fished out of a man's jewelry box containing no small fortune in gold. The charge built and Seamus swore the hair on his bare arms and legs was standing in response.

An audition, sure. One he planned to ace.

The building storm erupted in a cannonade of cymbals and snares, trilling guitar, and Seamus's on-point vocals. The first song on the list for their impromptu practice was the 3-D hit, "Body Language."

"*It wasn't what you said, but the way you said it,*" he sang. "*Within thirty seconds, you knew you'd get what you wanted; didn't have a doubt when my tongue went in and out. I wasn't from your country, babe, but I sure as hell spoke the language....*"

Seamus hit the high notes with unexpected ease, surprising even himself.

"Your lack of clothes didn't stop you from having baggage!"

The song ran out. Sweat poured down his neck. Seamus's nuts felt like lead ingots, hanging heavy beneath his root. He made a fist and punched air as the reverberations powered down. Hoots from his new bandmates replaced it.

"It's only one track, guys," Arif said.

"Yeah, but a hell of a track it was," Joe-Kev said, tapping his drumsticks together in applause.

Before lunch, they ran through "Little Red Wagon" and "Ghost Kisses," "Walk the Plank" and "Cemetery Road." Seamus faltered during the moody "In the Attic" and the rehearsal scratched to a stop, like that overplayed sound effect of record needle cutting across vinyl. They started again. Though he got through the song and hit the chords on the Fender guitar, it wasn't his best effort and Seamus knew it. Worse, so did the band.

"That's why it's called a practice," Shaye said.

They broke for lunch, which was served beside the pool. Seamus could barely believe his eyes at what the private caterer wheeled in—a platter of fresh fruit and berries, all of it looking more beautiful and colorful than anything he'd seen in grocery stores; seared prime rib finger sandwiches and a variety of condiments; salad; and an assortment of miniature pastries. Bottles of water and soda packed in ice filled a big metal trough.

"What, no beer?" Joe-Kev huffed.

Harley handed Seamus a plate. "You know how Duke feels about having alcohol present during official business."

"Maybe if he had a beer now and then, he'd be here enjoying himself instead of out there trying to find himself."

"That's enough," Harley said and the subject was dropped.

Seamus was hungry—how could anybody resist such a spread? Still, he wondered about Duke's strict no-alcohol edict.

As if picking up on his thoughts, Harley steered the discussion in another direction. "Normally, we keep a private chef on hand, but I'm going through one of our regular caterers to provide meals instead of having another person living here that we'll have to bring up to speed on the sitch with Duke."

Seamus loaded a pair of sandwiches onto his plate and spooned what he assumed was horseradish on the mahogany-colored beef. He tipped his chin toward the top-of-the-line grill sitting inert on the deck. "Why don't we just fire up that monster over there and cook some stuff ourselves?"

"Are you kidding?" Shaye chuckled, moving into line behind him. "We're 3-*fucking*-D, dude. We don't cook for ourselves; we get cooked for and served."

The drummer had said it in jest, but the lights went on at that moment for Seamus. He was still thinking like a pauper when he needed to act like a prince. A *duke*.

"Fucking-A," he said, and dumped the contents of his plate on the ground.

Let someone else clean it up.

He lounged with his bare feet kicked up, enjoying a cold soda. *Soda*. He didn't know how much power Harley wielded—quite a lot, he guessed—but Seamus vowed to change that policy banning alcohol from 3-D group gatherings. A little suds action wasn't going to hurt anyone or damage their style, if the afternoon's practice session was an indication of things to come. They'd nailed the song from *Spinal Column* and two more of the band's signature hits. He was, the new confidence in his head stated, *the man*.

Shaye strutted over to him and spread out on the nearest lounge chair. "Good work today."

"I know," the new monarch responded. Even to Seamus's ears, the answer sounded arrogant to a degree he couldn't imagine coming from his lips. Seamus Whyler was the kind of dude who normally thanked people and bowed.

From the corner of his eye, he caught the smirk on Shaye's face. "Just be sure you do it even better in San Diego."

San Diego, the first stop on the tour. In less than a week's time, he'd be on stage at Black's Music Hall, performing in front of thousands of screaming fanatics, all of them waiting to see his cock. Duke De Morte's, his inner voice reminded, suddenly less sure of itself.

"I'm not worried," he lied.

Shaye stretched. "I would be."

In the twenty minutes since breaking, Shaye had shed his shirt and pants and was now dressed only in a pair of dick-hugging bikini briefs. Seamus's mind absently wondered what the point of the scant underwear was; even at the periphery, he could see an enormous tube filled the pouch. Thick pubic curls bristled over the top of Shaye's waistband.

"*Duke* would be."

The statement brought them eye-to-eye.

"Huh?"

A little smirk formed on Shaye's lips. "The last time our boy Duke went in front of a live audience, none of us knew he was on the verge of a breakdown. Hell, he'd only started figuring it out for himself."

"Your point?"

"My point," Shaye said, reaching down and giving his cock a squeeze, "is that the last time the public saw Duke, he was shaking out the dregs of his jizz, his dong painted white. You should have seen it, dude."

"I did," Seamus said dryly.

"No, I mean in the flesh, no pun intended. There we are, at the end of the show. The audience is already creaming its jeans, in this fucking full-on frenzy. We're taking them down from it with "Europa"… like we just made them all bust, and now we're in the afterglow…and suddenly, there's Duke, jerking off. People start screaming. Hell, none of us knew what was going on. Arif, dude, he goes walking over to see what's causing such a ruckus, looks at the crowd, and he sees all these dudes out there in the audience with their hogs hanging out, *whacking it.* Bet you didn't see that part on your little computer."

Seamus shrugged and then tipped a glance down. The other man's hand was still on his cotton-covered dick. It wouldn't take much to open that package, and Seamus expected the keyboardist to whip it out if the conversation went on much longer.

"Arif looks over and there it is, big and white and leaking all over the fucking stage. It was like he'd blinked and found himself playing with the Chili Peppers instead of 3-D. Remember, we're all in fucking kilts, too. Dicks swinging and nuts hanging low and sweaty. Fuck, had he clued us in on what he planned to do, we all could have lifted and pumped for the crowd. By that point, you couldn't hear the music anyway."

Seamus's cocky new identity reasserted its pull. He settled back and grabbed hold of his meat, too. "So either you're trying to spook me by reminding me that I've got some big-ass shoes to fill… or a kilt, more to the point… or you're confessing you're jealous of the dude, 'cause he got to haul out his dick and the fans love him even more for it."

Seamus squeezed his meat, proud of its thickness. Suddenly, he liked the keyboardist a little less than a minute earlier after a day of sweating out the music together in the studio and bonding in the way good rehearsals tend to create good band members. He knew instantly what the man was trying to do—establish dominance by freaking him out. This wasn't so much a Seamus and Shaye thing at its core as a Duke and his keyboard player situation that went back to a time long before the big beating-off incident in Austin.

"Hey," Shaye barked, challenging his confidence. "Don't know how much of it you've been told to prepare you for this little *Vanilli* game by Duke and Harley, but I don't have anything to feel bad about."

The hand yanking on Shaye's underwear pulled harder. Shaye's cock slipped free of confinement, and Seamus couldn't help but be impressed.

"Whoa, dude," he sighed.

Two enormous balls spilled out beneath Shaye's dick. The cock standing above them, even half-erect, was magnificent to behold.

"So you see, buddy, don't try and make it like I was jealous of my good pal Duke just because he got to rub one out and give them the performance of a lifetime. I'm simply trying to be a friend to you by reminding you what you should expect out there at Black's Concert Hall. And I'm looking out for the band."

Seamus knew it was bullshit, but he thanked the other man anyway.

"Of course," Shaye said, his cocky smirk widening, his dick growing stiffer, "Duke and I did have a friendly little rivalry going."

"Oh?"

"Dick size. His snuck past mine, but only just. A fraction of an inch."

Seamus boldly tipped a look lower. The keyboardist's dick, thick and slightly curved, was fully hard now, rising up from all that pubic shag. The arrogant smirk on Shaye's face pushed his buttons. Reaching down, Seamus dropped the shorts to his knees. His cock slapped his six-pack with an audible *thwack* before jumping up to stand under its own power.

Shaye's eyes tracked his actions. Seamus gave his root a squeeze. The moist pink head of his cock popped out of his foreskin.

"No fucking way," Shaye said, all friendliness gone from his voice.

"Deal with it, dude," Seamus said, his place as Alpha dog once again secured. "Because while we didn't measure it with a ruler, I'd say I have a fraction on Duke, thanks to my foreskin."

Shaye scrambled up from the lawn chair. An instant later, the world went spinning out of focus as he yanked Seamus into the pool.

B-SIDE

Track 10

IT WASN'T MUCH, just a block of Swiss cheese, some crackers, a bunch of plump red seedless grapes, and icy sodas picked up at the little corner bodega, but arranged on the table it looked like a million bucks, straight out of a gourmet dining magazine. The candle Duke pulled off the kitchen windowsill, blackberry, completed the presentation.

"What do you think?" Duke asked, the nervousness in his voice clear. He shifted from one big foot to the other while waiting for Toby to answer. For a terrifying instant, he couldn't tell if the other man's wide-eyed expression was a good thing.

Then Toby smiled, and Duke's worry vanished. "It's perfect."

"I didn't have much on me," Duke said. The irony of it, when he considered how much money he had in no less than a dozen accounts, numerous investments, and hidden away in cash around the compound.

"I'd eat peanut butter sandwiches with you, and still think it the best date ever."

Duke reached for Toby's face and cupped his cheek. "You're incredible."

Toby leaned into his touch. "You, too."

"Now, about those peanut butter sandwiches."

They each took a seat around the spread, with Duke holding out Toby's chair, which seemed the proper thing to do. Duke unscrewed the cap of the soda bottle and poured both glasses full.

Toby raised his. "What should we toast to?"

Duke shrugged. "How about... Dan Fogelberg."

"To Dan. And Kurt Cobain. And Adam Yauch."

"Cheers," said Duke. "To John Lennon and George Harrison."

Their glasses chimed together.

"And to Ms. Whitney Houston, Donna Summer, and Laura Branigan."

"*I live among the creatures of the night,*" Duke hummed. "How about to Old Blue Eyes?"

"You remember Sinatra?"

"I'm a musician. Of course I do."

"To Sinatra. And... and... *Hell-vis*, to Elvis!"

"To Elvis, and three of the Brothers Gibb. To Levon Helm, may he keep on rocking in that big band in the sky. And the King of Pop for giving us 'Thriller.'"

Toby grinned. They toasted again.

"Yeah, to the music, and to the departed legends who made it so fucking great."

Toby reached for a cluster of grapes. Duke felt the other man's eyes wandering over him.

"You're so handsome."

Duke shook his head. "Stop it."

"You are."

"You're pretty fucking cute yourself, you know."

Toby shrugged. "It is what it is."

"What it is, dude, is fucking wonderful."

"Thanks. So?"

"So," Duke parroted. He pulled a slice of cheese and two crackers off the platter. "Since this is a real date, let's start with the Q & A. This place—rent or own?"

"Rent. It belongs to the guy that owns the Casino Club. He's got two other rentals in Bay Breeze. I get to walk to work, the rent's cheap, and it's a great little house."

"Perfect for fucking," Duke chuckled.

"That, too. What about you?"

Duke puffed a breath between his lips. "I've got a place in Beverly Hills. It's huge. Sometimes, I get lost in it. But there's a bungalow out back. It's where the band practices. We've even recorded in there. Our second album, *Absinthe and Arsenic*. It's like the band's clubhouse. I like that place. I get lost in there, too, but for the right reasons, I guess."

"Maybe, you should move the clubhouse into the main house and you move into the bungalow."

Duke raised both eyebrows. "There's a thought. I like your place."

"For real? You're so tall, it's just a matter of time before you knock your skull against an eave."

"Lucky for me, I have a thick skull."

Toby reached up and walked two fingers through Duke's hair. "Yup, real thick."

"Fuck you," Duke chuckled.

"Oh, you'd better. Fuck me hard."

Duke leaned across the table and their mouths met. The sweetness of the grapes on Toby's lips was intoxicating. "I intend to. And just so you're aware, more than once."

Toby rose from his seat. Using body language too clear to misinterpret, he guided Duke into the bedroom, leading him to the bed with a hand cupped over Duke's thickening cock. Once at their destination, Toby settled onto the edge of the mattress and unzipped Duke's jeans.

"Hell of a date so far," Duke growled, running his fingers through Toby's hair.

"So far—and it's still early," Toby said.

He sucked Duke's cock almost down to the hilt. Freeing his balls, Toby toyed with them, inspiring, to Duke's surprise, an old love ballad he hadn't heard played on the radio or a platter, cassette, CD, or download in ages. The melody of "Where is the Love" rose in the ether. As Toby swallowed him and yanked on his rocks, Duke hummed the Rita Coolidge and Billy Davis, Jr. tune.

Toby spit out Duke's cock. "Say what?"

A dreamy look in his eyes, Duke said, "Nothing, buddy. Don't stop what you're doing."

Toby resumed sucking Duke's cock.

Under his breath, Duke sighed, "It's here, that's where. The *love*..."

Duke eased Toby's boxer briefs off his ass. Some time ago, exploring similar territory between the halves of Harley's butt, Duke realized he was an ass man. He'd slept with plenty of women, liked sleeping with men a shade more, and while he was always the dominant male in any paradigm and, as such expected to be served more than to provide service, the one facet of dude-love he couldn't get enough of was eating a choice ass. While circling Toby's knot, he realized the other man had possibly ruined him for life. Toby Cosgrove owned the finest butt he'd ever feasted upon.

Duke licked the alphabet, upper case and lower, counted to one hundred, and still hadn't gotten enough. Throughout, Toby bucked beneath him, pinned under one of Duke's forearms. Humping his hard cock into the top sheet had created a slick puddle of precome. The musty smell triggered pent-up aggressions in Duke's psyche. He inserted a finger, grunted swears. Toby begged him to go deeper. Duke obliged.

Tongue first, finger second. Cock came next after he rolled a condom down his straining length. Duke eased in gently at first, making Toby aware of every inch, until he was in to his balls. Toby moaned beneath him and his voice sounded like music to Duke's ears, a song he would always remember.

The damp glistening on Toby's naked shoulders called to him. Duke leaned down and licked the other man's skin. Up his neck. Around his ear. Toby shuddered as much from his tongue as his dick, Duke imagined. The tight muscles sucking on his cock contracted, and Duke moaned, too.

"Your ass is so fucking *choice*," he huffed into Toby's ear. Then he nipped at the lobe and, unable to contain his lust, chewed on the corresponding length of throat.

"I love your cock in it," Toby gasped.

Duke drew back and pushed in, using his hips to deliver the thrust. A true and skilled cocksman, he gyrated, up and down, in and out, loving the loud slap of his balls as they bounced in concert with his movements, the sense of ownership—this was *his*.

The memory of he and Seamus Whyler tag-teaming Harley's ass, an ass he'd known intimately for years, flashed through his mind's eye. On the next slam into Toby, Duke's cock transformed from flesh into something with the consistency of steel. Seamus was like his twin, his reflection, and Duke had experienced zero jealousy in sharing Harley's asshole with him. In fact, having that extra dick grinding against his had heightened the experience into something more than a notch on a bedpost. A true bragging right, it had verged on supernatural in its intensity.

But thinking about Toby down on his knees slurping on Seamus in the dressing room at the Casino Club produced the complete opposite emotion. He never wanted Seamus to fuck Toby, because Toby was, well...

He reached down and grabbed hold of Toby's left ass cheek. "Who's is this?"

"Yours," Toby groaned.

"That's right."

Duke hauled his hips up so that only the head of his cock was still lodged in Toby's asshole. Maintaining that position for even a few minutes conjured fresh sweat.

"And who owns this dick of mine?" he demanded.

"I do, Duke. Duke's dick is mine, all mine."

"Fucking right, buddy. Duke's dick is all yours."

He slammed back in, knowing he was close, suspecting that Toby was as well. Was ownership proof of love? He couldn't be sure, but he knew how insane his emotions grew as he unloaded. Coming with Toby had an added layer to it that he'd never experienced before, not in all those other climaxes, in those many other choice asses.

They lay together in Toby's bed, the TV running in the background, tuned to the evening's baseball game. Boston was up two runs on Anaheim. The ocean crashed beyond nearby, perpetual and comforting white noise that filtered through the bedroom windows.

The last of the cheese and crackers vanished from the plate, leaving only the grapes. The ice cubes in Duke's sweating glass clinked, a reassuring counterpoint to the waves. The stale smell of sex between men hung over the room, mixing perfectly with the ocean's brine.

Duke studied Toby, watching the way he ate grapes and sipped his drink, only to find himself being studied in return.

"So tell me," Toby said.

"What do you want to know?"

"Everything."

Duke snorted a laugh. "That might take a while."

"I'm not in any hurry. My next band isn't set to show up until four o'clock tomorrow afternoon."

He ran his hand along the length of Duke's leg closest to him, an action Duke loved, though he flinched when Toby reached lower, past his ankle and onto his foot.

"Well, for starters, I'm ticklish."

"Too bad, dammit."

"Why?"

"Because you have sexy feet."

"Feet?" Duke lifted his size twelve, examined it. "Looks like a regular big ole man's foot to me, dude."

Toby slithered down and kissed his ankle, fingers wandering over toes and playing with them. "Oh, yeah—very sexy."

"You've got a foot fetish?" Duke asked.

"Call it what you want. There's just something insanely attractive about a handsome dude with big, bare feet. Yours are huge and, hate to break this to you, but you're the handsomest."

Flickers of passionate energy overtook Duke's nerves at having his foot played with. He eased his other from beneath the sheet and presented it to Toby. "You like my feet, buddy? They're all yours. Do with them what you want."

"Seriously?"

Duke answered with a smirk and a nod.

Toby's grin widened, and it pleased Duke to give the man something he not only craved but also clearly needed. It was worth the shivery sensations to see Toby's enthusiasm as his tongue moved between Duke's toes. The warm vacuum of his nostrils as they drank in the scent of his sweat was equally arousing. Nose and fingers and tongue explored him from instep to ankle, top to sole, toe to toe.

Duke's cock stiffened fully. He'd never had his feet worshipped and, to his surprise, he found that he liked it.

"*Fuck*," he sighed.

Toby ceased licking. "Am I doing something wrong?"

Duke gazed between his legs, down at his feet and the adorable face slobbering over them. "No, pal, you're doing everything right. Now get back to work and lick the sweat off my feet."

Duke jolted awake in the darkness, catching the gasp in his throat before it could spill past his lips. For a brief and startling moment, he didn't know where he was. Then he recognized the TV, still running, an infomercial scheme on how to get rich selling real estate playing on the screen. The soothing cadence of waves sounded beyond the windows.

Toby lay beside him in a nonclinging pose that made him adore the dude even more. This was a place easy to love, occupied by a guy he could say the same about.

Duke eased out of bed. Naked, his balls spilled down the furry inside of his thigh. His cock swung out half-hard above them, and he knew that if Toby were to stir and reach for his dick, he'd happily welcome his lips for a repeat performance of the most-excellent head that had followed the toe sucking.

Toby didn't, however, and Duke slipped free, grateful to be alone. Grateful that Toby let him. He strutted into the living room, catching a whiff of male sweat, the lingering odor of sex, and a hint of the blackberry candle as he passed.

He found a pad of paper and a pen, plunked his bare ass onto the beat-up but insanely comfortable sofa, and pulled the old guitar to his torso. The tune from his dream came clearly to him, without needing to be mined from his subconscious or forced back into the open. It poured out of his skull and tumbled down his arms, leapt off his fingertips, and onto the guitar strings.

Duke settled back against the cushions, arched one knee, an action that sent his balls spilling. His cock rested hotly against the other leg, still hard. Harder, judging by the itch along the sensitive trigger of nerves lining the underside of its head. Duke splayed his foot at an angle in the perfect position to be sucked on and sniffed, should Toby wander in.

He hadn't considered his feet sexy or remotely sexual until that night, but as with Toby's ass, he knew the dude had ruined him. Never again would Duke be able to live without having his toes serviced. He'd happily give Toby Cosgrove athlete's tongue, he thought with a chuckle.

He strummed lightly, aware of the late hour. *Early*, the little kitchen clock corrected. Stopping to jot down the chords, his straining cock demanded attention. Duke ignored it. He was hard over music, hard over the man sleeping soundly in the other bed.

The lyrics poured out of him, skull to fingers to the yellow legal pad's lined page.

What do you do when he's a dude, just like you? he wrote. *The guy that pushes all your buttons, makes you question all your sluttins'. What the hell are you gonna do when the right one's a dude, just like you?*

It was the first thing he'd written in months, and he knew it was good. Not only good, but it had the potential to be great. Duke scrawled the title "Bromance" above the chords and lyrics. If the band could handle skirting and flirting with that whole homoerotic factor so prevalent in Rock & Roll, it would be a major hit. Even the most hardened of college jocks would howl it to the limits of their lungs at keg parties and frat house initiations. It would boom over stadiums between innings of baseball games. Closeted he-men everywhere would jerk their dicks to it, and a bold contingent would find the strength within themselves to wander out of closets and into the open, taking pride in their true identities.

Much like Duke had.

A rush of joy swept through him, icy-hot in intensity. The music... *his* music. How the hell had he lived this long, judged as being successful by everyone around him and by all outward signs, but never having experienced this updraft of euphoria before now?

"Hey," asked a sleepy voice from the bedroom door.

Duke glanced up, and the happy look on his face deepened. Toby stood in the doorway, naked and erect, arms folded in a charming, jaunty pose.

Duke set the guitar and legal pad aside. "Come here," he said, giving in to the needs of his dick.

Track 11

SEAMUS HIT THE water awkwardly and took a bitter sip of pool cocktail heavy with chemicals. His shorts formed a figure-eight noose around his ankles. He kicked free of them while breaking the surface. Chlorine burned somewhere between his throat and his sinuses. The water's temperature did little to cool his rage.

Shaye bobbed on the surface directly behind him, anger written across his face. Luckily, they were in the deep end. The water cushioned their plunge, keeping them from breaking bones or worse. It also stopped them from throwing punches.

"What the fuck?" Seamus demanded.

Another voice answered, from somewhere near the line of citrus trees. Seamus tipped a look in that direction and watched Arif amble over, his cell phone clutched in one hand. He set it and his sunglasses down on one of the upright lounge chairs.

"Nobody invited me into the pool."

"Come on in," Shaye said casually, as though the spilled chairs and two naked dudes bobbing up and down in the deep end were the most natural thing in the world. "Clothing is optional."

"Yeah, I see that," Arif said, giving them a tip of his chin. He peeled off his shirt, kicked off his sneakers. In short order, he yanked off socks, a pair of maroon-colored briefs, and stood only in his chains and watch. The watch, an expensive gold beaut with a ring of sapphires around the clock face, joined his phone at poolside.

Hooting out a loud war cry, Arif cannonballed into the pool, his dick and balls helicoptering as he plummeted. By the time the column of displaced water fell, Joe-Kev and Harley were out of the main house.

"My invitation get lost in the mail?" Joe-Kev grumbled.

Without waiting to be asked, he stripped, baring that impressive canvas of inked muscles. One, in particular, drew Seamus's attention—the grinning phantom face tattooed across the top of the handsome fucker's tool.

"Dude, is that a human skull on your dick?"

Joe-Kev grunted an affirmative beneath his breath, gave his cock a shake, and jumped in. Harley was the last one to join the group, and then much spirited laughter, splashing, and fucking about ensued. Arif performed an elegant dive off the board, his dick swinging. Joe-Kev followed, less gracefully, though Seamus was hypnotized by the dude's body, which put Henry Rollins's and the Edge, the hot Irish guitarist's from U2 to shame.

Whatever weird shit Shaye had attempted to pull with him got temporarily shelved, until Seamus caught him staring from the cut of his eye, smiling through clenched teeth, his expression like a live version of the grinning skull on Joe-Kev's dick.

He flipped the steaks, jumping back when a burst of smoke and sizzle erupted from the grill.

"Careful, don't burn your balls off," Arif said.

Seamus stood at the top-of-the-line grill, naked except for his chef's apron.

"And don't get your balls on my meat," Shaye said.

Seamus shot a cocky smirk at the four men lounging naked around the patio. "Funny, you didn't have a problem with that before."

The dudes chuckled, all save their drummer.

Following their naked romp in the pool, Seamus had suggested finally putting the inert grill to use—what was the purpose of having one if it sat there collecting dust, he'd reasoned. Harley got on the phone and in half an hour, a case of choice steaks had arrived at the front gate from the caterer, along with salads, leafy and potato, and a case of ice-cold beer.

"But—?" Harley had protested at that last part of the order.

"This isn't official 3-D business. It's a cookout, so chill," he'd said, and that had been that. Seamus was starting to walk the walk and liked it. He was the Top Nut now, the man in charge and clearly the one with the biggest cock. The duke of this domain.

Seamus raised the beer to his lips. Walking around naked with his balls bouncing low and his mighty dick proudly displayed was empowering. He noticed plenty of roaming eyes openly sizing up the competition. The uncrowned winner of the contest, even limp, was shielded behind a dark green *Kiss the Cook* apron. No wonder Shaye got pissed—even their Duke Dalton ringer's dick was bigger. Shaye could kiss the cook and his cock.

He pulled the steaks off the grill and arranged them on a platter. Dark and juicy, the aroma wafting up made his stomach growl. How long had it been since he'd eaten a steak? Even a cheap, chewy cut? He could eat steaks five times a day now if he wanted. Ten. A million.

Seamus whipped off the apron, unaware that he'd gotten stiff until he started toward the patio with the platter held atop the fingers of one hand, waiter-style. The aching swell bobbed proudly in front of him. *Fuck it*, he thought. Let them all see his cock, big as a stallion's, with its extra folds of skin. Let 'em look. He was a duke among men.

"Steak's up," Seamus said.

"So's the *tube steak*," Harley said.

Grinning, Seamus set the platter beside the salads and reached for another beer. After dinner, he'd give Harley a taste of some tube steak, for sure.

Beer, steaks, money… and instant sex, whenever he wanted it. Seamus was starting to think how easy it would be to get used to this life. A million bucks sure sounded great when he was lucky to have twenty in his pocket. But Duke Dalton had multitudes of millions.

Duke had Harley.

Duke had the contracts, the endorsements.

Duke had the life.

"Eat up," Seamus said.

He planned to have the life, too, whether it was for six weeks, six months, or forever. As much as he liked the guy, a growing part of Seamus secretly wished the real Duke Dalton had gotten lost in his quest for happiness and that he wasn't coming back.

A KNOCK SOUNDED on the bedroom door.

Seamus closed the closet. While rummaging around among Duke's collection of sneakers, he found a shoebox containing fifty grand in hundred-dollar bills. Another ten thousand lurked at the back of one of Duke's three sock drawers. Seamus mentally noted these things for future reference.

Clearing his throat, aware of the fresh, damning sweat dripping from his hairline, proof of his guilt, Seamus answered the door.

"Harley," he sighed. Only it wasn't.

The rough, handsome face of Joe-Kev Hallet greeted him.

"Dude, I thought—"

"Yeah, I gathered that," Joe-Kev said, marching into the room with his hands in his pockets.

Seamus closed the door. "Come on in."

Joe-Kev narrowed one eye on him in response to the snark. The black tank the drummer had donned following their skinny dip in the pool and their naked barbecue looked like it had been spray-painted over his inked chest muscles. The cargo shorts showcased perfect legs. Even Joe-Kev's baseball hat, turned backward, and his sneakers, minus socks, added to the powerful image. Seamus caught a hint of pool chemicals mixed with clean, masculine sweat. Suddenly, he struggled to breathe.

"What... uh... can I help you with, dude?"

"Nothing," Joe-Kev answered.

A man of few words, thought Seamus. Your typical Rock & Roll tough guy. Only nothing about Joe-Kev seemed typical. He looked like he'd be more at home on a football team's offensive line or in a dusty Army uniform, overseas in some desert, instead of making music in a band.

"Then to what do I owe the honor of this visit?"

God, that sounded toity. A voice in Seamus's head reminded him that only a few days earlier, he was washing up in a gas station restroom and sleeping in his car. An unexpected pang jolted him back to the car, to his guitar, his scrapbook. The emotion was powerful, painful.

"I meant—" Seamus started to say.

"It's okay," Joe-Kev said. "You're busy."

The other man returned to the door. As he passed, Seamus drew in more of his scent and it was, his inner voice proclaimed, as magnificent as hitting the high note, nailing the performance, and bringing the crowd to its feet in applause.

"Wait," he called.

Joe-Kev froze at the open door but didn't turn.

"Seriously, dude. *Joe-Kev*," Seamus said, stressing the man's name. "You need anything?"

"Yeah, I do, but it's cool if you don't got time."

And then he exited the room, leaving Seamus alone in a borrowed house, in a rented skin, wondering what the fuck had just happened.

HE DIDN'T GO after Joe-Kev, when every register in his skull, his soul, and his balls told Seamus that he should. The guys departed, all except Arif, who'd downed too many suds and was passed out in one of the house's many guestrooms. That, too, broke Duke's laws.

And Harley reminded him of that fact. "We do keep drivers and vehicles on hand."

"I know. I've peeked into that hanger you call a garage," Seamus fired back from the bed, where he casually yanked aside his shorts, allowing his balls to spill out. "There's what, like a dozen souped-up cars in there?"

"There are eight. The others are in storage."

Seamus rolled his eyes. "Anyway..."

"Anyway, pal, there are reasons we don't drink during group business, and that includes get-togethers like that impromptu cookout you held. And we don't normally allow band members to crash here overnight."

"Why not? You do."

"That's different."

Seamus worked his cock out. "How's that any different than letting the bass player sleep it off in the west wing?"

"Technically, that room's in the *east* wing," Harley said, dropping his folded arms. He sauntered over to the bed and lowered for a taste. After several stiff sucks on Seamus's dick, he added, "Duke likes to keep things professional, all business all the time."

Seamus thought about how even Harley's oral services were starting to feel all business, all the time—no different than signing a contract or negotiating some new deal. The dude was great at it, no complaints. He gave Seamus's nuts a tug while resuming the expert skills he'd already shown on his nine straining inches. Only now that Seamus realized Harley's affection was simply another part of the job description, no more and no less, he struggled to enjoy it.

Closing his eyes, Seamus thought about Joe-Kev's visit, and his mind wandered. What if Duke hadn't been all business, and had fooled around within the band with someone other than Harley? Only Harley wasn't wise to it? "*Wow*," Seamus exclaimed.

"You like that, dude?" Harley asked, misinterpreting the statement.

Sensing it better to agree, Seamus did.

Duke and Joe-Kev. It wasn't your usual pairing of tall and tough with shorter and slighter, top and bottom, the strong and masculine dude with the guy expected to fill the effeminate role, like the classic scenario unfolding between Seamus's spread legs. Guys like Seamus and Duke were expected to have their needs serviced by dudes who got off on giving the service, men like Harley and the one who'd gone down at him back at the Casino Club. What was his name? Rory? For an instant, Seamus couldn't remember. *Toby.*

A rugged he-man like Joe-Kev stood proudly in the same physical ranks as Seamus and Duke. Did his hard exterior shield a soft, sensitive center? Seamus didn't think it possible. Still, that excited whiff of testosterone among the sweat and pool chemicals, and the way Seamus's internal chemistry had reacted, was far more brilliant than the robotic hum-job Harley was giving him, no matter how professional.

Joe-Kev. A light went off, and with it came an updraft of emotion and arousal. Were they secret lovers? So secret that Duke's right-hand Dude Friday didn't know? His bandmate was a warrior, a *Viking*, a force of fucking nature. All that ink. Seamus remembered the skull tattooed on Joe-Kev's dick and couldn't hold back. Shudders racked his body. His dick unloaded. Howling, he glanced down, only it wasn't Harley the efficient personal assistant sucking on his beast; it was their drummer, so masculine and magnificent, he challenged everything Seamus believed about his cock and, more importantly, his heart.

The man walked into the room, and Seamus felt the temperature skyrocket. Joe-Kev greeted him with a darting glance and a tip of his chin.

"Dude," Seamus answered in response.

He searched for a trace of the other man's scent, but the heady mix of male hormones and pool chemicals was gone, driven out by the odor of alcohol leaching through Arif's pores and a cloying cologne Shaye had splashed on, likely to disguise some other stink beneath. The concept of being locked in the studio with that mixture for an entire day nauseated him. But knowing Joe-Kev was there made it doable.

Harley handed out the day's schedule, a sheet containing the songs they would run through, including notes about which ones needed the most work. More business. No wonder Duke had suffocated in this environment.

He ran an eye over the page. It was the same order as the previous day's playlist. They took their positions. Seamus sang and the band played.

Three days later, to Harley's dismay, Seamus crumpled up the playlist and roared, "For Chrissakes, guys, can we shake this up a bit? Why don't we open with "Red Alert" or do something totally fucking off the cuff and completely unexpected—like a cover of "Sailing" by Christopher Cross?"

"Are you fucking out of your mind?" Shaye asked.

"Yeah, dude, I am. *Bored* out of it. Where's the fun, the excitement?"

"Maybe it's back in that big, kick-ass career you had playing at two-bit clubs before you were given the chance to jam with us, *yo*."

White-hot rage pulsed through Seamus's insides. He didn't remember throwing the first punch, just the last, right before Joe-Kev stepped between the two men, effortlessly putting an end to the fisticuffs.

The tremor in the air started building during that short but ugly clash, not a full week behind them. Like magma pooling underground, creating heat and friction, readying to explode from the volcano's caldera as lava and devastating everything in its path.

The entire world trembled. The air shook. Seamus's heart raced.

"We ready to do this?" Shaye asked.

The men nodded and, in sequence, committed.

"Let's do it," Seamus said.

He caught his reflection in the mirror, and it all became real. The crisp black and white attire fit him to perfection and hadn't required a single alteration. Duke De Morte's black shoes, too. He could tell by the look in Perry's eyes that even the trusted makeup artist couldn't believe the resemblance.

The band exited the dressing room. The crowd's roar doubled in intensity. Seamus had never heard anything so loud; so *dick-stiffening wonderful.*

The three other men, dressed as their alter egos, raced ahead of him, past the curtains and security guards and onto the stage. The cacophony became deafening, but it paled when Duke De Morte adjusted his cock, choked down the last of his hesitation, and charged out after them.

The volcano erupted, and 3-D blew the crowd away.

Track 12

"THAT SOUND MEANS there's a world of hurt—and it's coming from her mini-skirt. Red Alert! Red Alert!"

There were seconds when Seamus worried that his voice had shorted out and died on him. But it was only the crowd's orgiastic loudness, thousands of horny human bodies driven into frenzy by the chance to see 3-D in the flesh after six months of laying low. 3-D yes, but Duke De Morte, Duke Dalton and his dick, more than anyone or anything associated with the concert.

He sang, intending for his voice to reach every corner, every person in the crowd, aware of the looseness of his balls, the heaviness in the front of his pants, and the power he possessed. He was Duke. Hell, he was a *king*. Dare he think it? A god?

"When you hear the klaxon-cries, like on the Starship Enterprise, *run and grab your gun—Red Alert!"*

The opening performance ended where it began—with the audience on its feet, screaming. *Coming,* thought Seamus. His hard-on stood noticeably, and he couldn't remember a time this exciting, this happy. He grabbed his dick, which brought even more adoration from the audience, and then the microphone.

"Hello, San Diego!"

Shrieks and hoots answered.

"You're one hot-as-fuck, fine-looking group, and it is our mother-fucking honor to play for you on this sweaty summer night."

Seamus bowed. He owned the audience, the biggest he'd ever played to. He could have stuck his rod in any hole out there, dudes as well as ladies. If he never felt the rush of supremacy again—

He hesitated from belting out the song from *Spinal Column* because he wanted to absorb the memory of that instant.

Then Seamus sensed the others waiting for him to segue into the band's famous film anthem, made a fist, pumped air, and reached for the Fender.

Showtime.

They ran through the first ten songs with ease. Joe-Kev's stirring drum solo in

"Little Red Wagon" kept Seamus's dick in its hardened state, right in time for intermission.

His pulse raced. The moment of truth was fast approaching.

Seamus eased out of the zombie jacket and kicked off his shoes, his eyes locked on the kilt without blinking. The anticipation of this next half hour of the show had turned the crowd into a restless mob with itchy camera fingers. Would he do it or not? Seamus was fucked if he knew the answer.

"Hey, dude," called a voice from the door.

Seamus turned. There, Perry stood.

THE SPIRITED ROCK & Roll song "Chop Shop" crescendoed in a screech of guitars and tribal drumbeats. The strobe lights cut out, leaving absolute darkness. The screams died, too, and the audience held its breath. The black lights lit. Four ghostly faces appeared on the stage, hovering disembodied in the haze of dry ice fog.

Arif and Seamus began to play the opening chords of the moody instrumental "Europa," and the crowd again went collectively mad in anticipation.

Shaye Floden, known onstage as the creature Bones, temporarily abandoned his keyboard for the sax and belted out the sultry section of that instrument's solo, during which the infamous act had taken place six months earlier.

Seamus's cock still tingled from being hand-painted in the phosphorescent white, made up by Perry's groping fingers. Plucking on the guitar, he made a half-circle around his bandmates, strolling past Shaye and then Joe-Kev—amazing Joe-Kev—before cycling back to Arif. The two men strummed and gyrated in perfect formation, creating pure sex together, only with guitars instead of gonads.

He wasn't sure he could do it. And then he realized he had to. Seamus unstrapped himself from the guitar and set it on the stand. The screams rose to their most deafening yet. Unburdened from his fear, Seamus lifted his kilt and his massive white dick jutted proudly into view.

Eyes half-closed, and with the audience going psycho, he stepped closer to the precipice and let it happen. For a week, he hadn't required Harley's oral services and had only jerked off once over the past three days. He didn't need Harley anymore, he'd told himself throughout. Besides, he wanted to save it up, just in case he found the balls to go through with it, which he had.

Still, while masturbating and with thousands of phone cameras flashing and people trying to get past security for a better look or, hell, a *taste*, he thought of Harley. And of Duke's hard cock pumping against his while buried together in Harley's can. And, curiously, he thought of Wanda, who hadn't entered his consciousness in some time. He was licking her pussy, tasting her sweet honey; fucking her doggy-style, in that bed, in that house in Winter Woods. And then, with the soulful instrumental about to reach its climax, he thought about Joe-Kev. Seamus's low-swinging balls drew upward, and the world went out of focus in a rush of happy energy.

A ribbon of spunk sailed out of his cock and into the crowd. Four more shots followed, with both dudes and women either diving out of the way or jumping over the backs of their fellow concertgoers while attempting to get a sample of his DNA.

The junk they thought was Duke Dalton's.

Seamus shook out his cock, lowered his kilt, and rejoined the band. They took two encores, playing to thousands that seemed on the verge of passing out, and delivering, as one rock critic in the crowd put it, the best concert of the year.

At the time, none of 3-D or the band's crew realized that Marquis Stilton was in the second row, center, taking it all in with a sharp eye and an even sharper camera.

"That was fucking great," Seamus said. He made a fist and pumped air. His black combat boots matched the moves with a coordinated boxer's fancy footwork.

Apart from the boots and a length of black wool sock visible above the tops, the only remaining stitch on Seamus's entire body was the kilt. He'd shed the shirt, tie, and tuxedo jacket following the melee after that final bow. Even after ejaculating what felt like a gallon of whitewash into the crowd, Seamus's dick refused to go down. It jumped with his jabs and dance moves. He wanted to fuck. He wanted to scream. So this was what stardom felt like?

"Great job, guys," Harley said.

Unable to control himself, Seamus picked up the band's brains and swung him around. Once planted firmly again on the ground, Seamus pecked a sloppy kiss on Harley's cheek, leaving a smear of white.

"Stop it," Harley chuckled. "At least until after makeup removal!"

Seamus remembered his cock, still slathered in the same white mess as his face. Yes, he wanted to fuck. To fuck and to drink and to fuck some more.

The usual parade of groupies taken in by invitation was missing. The band couldn't risk having their ruse unmasked by some horny piece of tail with an eagle's eye.

"Makeup removal, sure," Seamus said.

He needed to channel the energy somehow, and he didn't think the bowls of candy or bottles of spring water would do it. It didn't occur to him until he was seated in the chair dressed only in a towel and Perry was removing the white from his face that always before, the simple act of making music had been enough. Playing to houses containing a total of ten bodies had, in the past, done the same for him as tonight's orgasming thousands.

The scrapbook. Seamus hadn't thought about it in days, but suddenly the urge to hold it up and flip ahead to the first blank sheet, to stick in a ticket stub or a folded-over poster, possessed him. He was halfway out of the makeup chair before Perry's voice snapped him back to reality.

"Whoa, amigo, please sit your ass down until I'm done."

"But—"

"No buts, just your *butt*."

Perry removed the last of the white paint from his face and then slapped Seamus's towel-clad ass. Seamus opened the towel and let it drop, his mind still consumed with grabbing some memento from the show. He had a keepsake from every gig he'd ever played, dating back to the very beginning. That tiny length of blue fishing line behind the first page's plastic sleeve now seemed like a relic from a different universe, but the thread connected all the way to this night, this rush, in a clean, straight line. Without the fencepost and fishing line guitar, there would be no 3-D for him, no frenzied crowd, no dick painted ghostly white.

Pins and needles surged over his skin and deeper, through his blood, as Perry lifted the aching lump of his cock. Suddenly, Seamus was back in the chair, focused on the present. And in the present, he was sitting on a towel, completely naked, having his stiff dick swabbed with a makeup removal sponge by another dude.

"Incredible, man," Perry sighed, his words raining heat down across Seamus's crotch.

Perry wiped off more of the stage paint. Pink flesh appeared among the white.

"Thanks," Seamus said. It seemed the appropriate response.

"No, seriously, I don't think I'm betraying some sacred vow by telling you that I put the white on Duke, so I've been in this position before."

"Position? You mean down between his legs?"

Perry nodded. "His cock is...*damn*, let's just say that he's got a hell of a dick."

I know, thought Seamus. But on that point, his tongue remained silent.

Perry's fingers glided along the underside of his shaft and tickled the sensitive trigger of nerves lining the base of the head. Seamus tensed. His cock thrust forward, and a shiver tumbled down his spine.

"Your cock," Perry continued, and Seamus was aware of the other man's fingers intimately, all of them on his cock, not just in a professional capacity but playing with it, working it toward the big release Seamus so desperately needed.

"Your cock, too...it's a fucking work of art."

Seamus spread his legs, no longer worried about professionalism. "You like it so much, why don't you prove it by showing me the same respect you gave Duke."

"Thought you'd never ask," Perry said.

The dude's grip on his dick tightened. Seamus settled back and closed his eyes. Breathless seconds later, Perry's tongue brushed his sac. Then, one at a time, his balls vanished into the other man's mouth.

He thought of the insane inspiration of being on stage, and of the freedom he'd so often dreamed about while playing one shitty gig or another. So many lousy gigs, one bar or club or lame street fair after another. So many matchbook covers and napkins. He would never go back to that. Never. Anything that found its way into the scrapbook from this night forward would be total big time.

"Yeah, lick my nuts, dude...."

Perry licked, and Seamus busted his second load of the night, this one privately to an audience of two.

The tour bus rolled on, headed north to San Francisco. Seamus glanced at the clock. Eleven past three in the morning. The smoothness of rolling wheels lulled him to a place that wasn't quite sleep but a transcendental state through which the events of the night played and replayed as phantom images superimposed over the surrounding bunks.

Perry had exited the dressing room licking his lips, Seamus imagined. Still naked and in need of a shower, he'd moved to close the door. And there, standing outside with his hands stuck in his pockets, was Joe-Kev. The man of few words didn't offer any, but Seamus didn't need words to recognize the drummer's expression.

Seamus had hovered as much behind the door as possible. "Hey."

Joe-Kev avoided his eyes and chin-tipped him.

"What's up?"

"Just wanted to say you did a fucking great job out there."

"You, too, man," Seamus said. "I was just gonna grab a shower. You want to come in?"

Come in, because whatever else had happened on this fuck-tastic night and despite nutting live on stage and into Perry's face courtesy of the lead makeup man's jerking fingers, the vision of Joe-Kev Hallet would give him cause to get stiff again with shocking ease.

Only Joe-Kev shook his head and walked away, and a shadow of guilt helped by equal parts confusion swept over him.

The bunk on the tour bus was more comfortable than his car, but after a week's worth of night's crashing at the compound in Beverly Hills, Seamus couldn't get comfortable. Maybe it was the adrenalin. Like his mind, his pulse refused to come down fully from the excitement. He and the band were headlining at the Circus for two nights. Two more chances to drive the crowd mad. Given the stiffness of his cock, he doubted there'd be a problem showing them the same treatment as the audience in San Diego.

Seamus glanced over to the lower bunk across from his. A length of hairy leg and a big foot with a tiger's face inked across the top hung out of the covers. Joe-Kev's snores reached him through the white noise of wheels running asphalt. With Shaye asleep above Joe-Kev, Arif, he assumed, dozing overhead, and Harley up near the front, lounging on a bench, all he wanted to do was crawl into bed beside that leg and foot, feel the strength in the muscles of the man they belonged to, and enjoy the warmth of another soul who understood what he was experiencing. The music, the rush, the dick-hardening power of it all.

Instead, Seamus suffered alone, listening to Joe-Kev's breaths and the wheels traveling beneath them, banshee music that made him long for his old guitar.

THE SHOW AT the Circus was a rousing success, judging by the reception they received from the fans. While Seamus could have done a better job with the soundtrack song, he hit all the right high notes leading up to it, and with the much-anticipated "Europa" approaching, the audience grew louder and rowdier, masking most of his *Spinal Column* mistakes.

The lights dimmed. The black lights switched on, creating the zombie-faced phantoms on stage. Seamus's cock had been painted white during the costume change, leaving him well aware of its hardness bobbing heavily over his balls. He was ready. Duke De Morte would unload his skeet into the audience, which was clamoring for him to give them the same thrill as the crowds in Austin and San Diego.

But, while gyrating around the stage, he caught a look at the band's drummer, the ghoul named Autopsy, and the notion of ejaculating into the crowd felt like betrayal.

Seamus marched back toward Arif, who handled the song's guitar demands magnificently. He bowed to the crowd, which screamed even louder, waiting for his hard white cock to make its appearance.

Instead of giving them the thrill they craved, Seamus resumed playing his guitar. As the instrumental continued and it became clear that Duke De Morte wasn't planning to lift his kilt, the aroused chants turned to boos, and the Heaven he'd experienced at the previous concert degenerated on this night into pure Hell.

Track 13

THEY'D FUCKED. ONLY in the aftermath of the near-violent dance across Toby's bed, Duke thought of it as *lovemaking*, because he loved Toby, and Toby loved him in return.

The afternoon air pouring in through the windows stirred the sweaty tang of sex. So much sex—only a single day in the previous week had passed without Duke's cock vanishing into one end of Toby or the other, and that only because they'd spent the afternoon at the beach, enjoying the sun and the surf. A dinner of burgers on the grill and a movie off pay-per-view had followed. Even without the divine tightness of Toby's throat and ass, it was one of the best days of Duke's life.

Clad only in a pair of Seamus Whyler's frayed boxer briefs, Duke flipped through the scrapbook. He didn't understand why his alter ego had chosen a coil of dirty blue fishing line as a keepsake to be preserved at the beginning of his personal catalog of recorded history, but he assumed it was important; some vital relic upon which everything else archived in the scrapbook's pages was built upon.

Toby appeared at the living room door, dressed similarly, the clean fragrance of his recent shower carrying close enough for Duke to inhale. "Hey."

"Hey, babe," Duke said, uncrossing his feet

Toby folded his arms. "You're reading that book again?"

"Obviously," Duke said lightly.

"I'm curious why?"

Duke glanced down at the pages in front of him. One was a flyer for a high school talent show, clearly printed from someone's home computer. The clipping across from it was out of the school's newspaper and reported that Seamus Whyler's band had taken the top prize. A few similar clips carried through college, and then the matchbooks and cocktail napkins began to appear behind plastic sleeves, an endless succession of reminders.

"You can tell that it's the one other thing besides his guitar that Seamus loves. Truly loves, because he's earned it. He owns what's in this book."

Duke closed the scrapbook and slapped the patch of leg above his knee, beckoning Toby over. Toby obeyed and planted his ass on Duke's lap. The two men hugged and shared a short but powerful kiss.

"You smell great," Duke growled.

"So do you."

"I stink," Duke chuckled.

"Yeah, like I said, you smell great."

Duke's cock stirred. "Don't do this to me, dude. You've already drained me twice today."

"So, do you have enough left in you for *round three*?"

Having Toby on his lap was fast becoming torturous. "Maybe," he growled, flashing a mischievous smirk.

Toby crushed his mouth over Duke's a second time while shifting his position. The combination sealed it.

"Oh yeah, round three," Duke sighed.

Toby slid down and spread Duke's legs. By then, Duke's cock was thick in his underwear and he was eager for it to be serviced. Toby took him halfway down his shaft while he played with Duke's balls.

"Fuck, dude," Duke said. He tossed back his head and savored the attention, but his mind cycled back to the scrapbook.

Toby's phone rang. He hopped up to answer it.

For this latest go around, Duke had shuffled over to the sofa and now, naked and spent, lounged with his bare feet kicked up on one of the sofa's arms. He reached for the scrapbook. About halfway in was a photo of Seamus and an attractive blonde woman. He was strumming on the guitar, seated on a stool, in that classic music-man pose. The blonde stood beside a microphone and though the snapshot had frozen her in time, Duke knew that she was warbling some tune in concert with Seamus playing. It was the sort of photo that looked like it came off a disposable camera, one probably left on a table at a wedding reception to record the event. A matchbook cover tucked beside the photo, decorated in gold-leaf whirls that bore the words *Wedding of Cassandra Coltrane to Blake Foley*, confirmed the theory.

Duke hesitated, because it felt wrong. Then, he remembered that Seamus was sleeping in his bed, jerking off on his high-thread-count sheets, eating on his expense account, and likely fucking his assistant at both of Harley's choice ends. So he lifted the plastic sleeve, picked out the photograph, and turned it around. *Seamus and Wanda* was written on the back, along with a date. Duke did the math. Six years ago.

He returned the photograph. While flipping pages, a letter in a pastel purple envelope slipped out. The return address was from Wanda Cofield, from Winter Woods, New Hampshire. The date on the cancelled stamp wasn't long after that on the back of the photograph.

"Shit," Toby said behind him.

"What is it?"

"My Bon Jovi tribute band is stuck in Jersey with a flat tire, so now I'm down an act. Do you feel like filling in for them tonight?"

Duke absorbed the unexpected twist. "As...?"

"As our old reliable standby, Seamus Whyler. There's two hundred bucks in it for you, plus a meal. What do you say, dude?"

Duke felt his balls constrict as Toby's offer plunged them into an imaginary bucket filled with water and ice cubes. Perform alone on stage, under an assumed identity? Whipping out his dick and pumping it to climax in front of thousands of fans hadn't terrified him so much. Stage fright? Thinking those words, the name of his father's old band, didn't help.

"Uh..." he yammered.

"Come on, tough guy," Toby pleaded. He grabbed hold of Duke's right foot by the ankle and massaged it from instep to toes in loving caresses. "You can do it, and you'd be saving my ass. I can always play CDs, but our patrons are expecting a live show tonight. It's just one night—and Bon Jovial will be back on the road and here in time for tomorrow. You'd be yanking my ass out of the fire."

Duke reached out and grabbed Toby, who'd wiggled that burning ass into loose-fitting black shorts post-coitus. "I can't let this ridiculously smoking-hot butt get scorched, can I?"

He yanked down Toby's shorts, baring his ass, and sunk his teeth playfully into Toby's left cheek. Toby hooted in protest. Forcing his mouth away from Toby's can took Herculean effort. Duke squeezed both halves, one in each hand, and then released him. If Toby remained in his clutches much beyond that, he'd be tempted to eat that incredible asshole for hours, unable to resist.

"So?"

"Yes, dammit," Duke agreed.

Panic threatened to overwhelm him, the first true case of the shakes he'd felt in decades. Hell, even when a six-year-old Duke Dalton had raced onto the stage at one of his dad's band's concerts with a fake wig of curls twice his height, he'd loved the audience's cheers—an audience considerably bigger than anything he could expect to face tonight at the Casino Club.

Shit, he thought, that was the problem. The intimacy of playing such a venue. There'd be no security guards, no media, far fewer cameras, if any. It would be just him and them and the music.

Duke swore under his breath, jumped from the sofa, and made it to the porcelain throne one step ahead of his rising gorge.

HE STARED AT his reflection in the dressing room mirror. A little ashen in the face and red in the eyes, but otherwise fine, thought Duke.

"How do I look?"

Toby's reflection joined his in the mirror. "I'd say even hotter than the last time you performed for the Casino Club set, Mister Whyler."

Toby smacked his ass—hard. Duke jumped.

"Hey, now! I'm the ass man in this bromance."

He seized hold of Toby's wrists and wrestled him into the nearest corner. Their lips met. So did their groins. Duke gave a grinding push before pulling away. Much more of that and he'd miss his curtain call.

"You're gonna be great," Toby said. He stole one more kiss before he exited the dressing room ahead of Duke.

The walk to the stage was the longest of Duke's professional career. Duke Dalton had played for crowds of tens of thousands in LA, New York, Paris, London, Berlin, Sydney, Buenos Aires, Tokyo, and Hong Kong. But taking the simple wooden stool for three dozen beachgoers in Bay Breeze, New Hampshire unleashed a kind of panic that nearly crippled him. He was sweating clots and his hands shook. Duke imagined that his nuts had shriveled into raisins.

It was the closeness that shocked him so. He could see their faces, smell their perfumes and colognes. The music and the musician were accessible in ways that Duke had never experienced.

And then the thought at the heart of his worry flashed clearly through his consciousness.

What if I'm not good enough?

A fraction of the applause he was used to hearing rose around him in the subdued glow of candlelit tables. The two spotlights trained upon him were low level in their intensity but seemed, in his panic, to be as bright as anything strobing the sky above the red carpet at a Hollywood premiere. He did a quick sound check. Everything was perfect apart from Duke's racing heart.

"Good evening, folks," he said casually. "It's great to be here again, and it's my pleasure to perform for you tonight. Because this is a night that was made for music."

He started to strum. And sing.

Duke's worry evaporated.

Earlier in the afternoon, after quelling his nausea, Duke had hastily thrown together a selection. He opened with a cover of "Summer Breeze" by Seals and Crofts.

And, just like the lyrics, he was feeling fine. Because of the music, and the small yet intimate crowd and the connection he made with them. Following "Summer Breeze," he improvised "Laura" from the classic Film Noir, which every great solo performer from Sinatra to Mathis to Carly Simon had made their own, then belted out "Blackbird" by the Beatles and, more recently, Sarah McLachlan, and Kenny Loggins's "I'm Alright." The brilliant and moody Steely Dan hit "Deacon Blues" sounded great even without the saxophone, performed by a band of one, and he earned a standing ovation when he ended the first set with "Georgia on my Mind."

Chills cascaded up and down his spine. Duke took a bow. He could hardly wait to get back to the music. His music… why had he never felt this passionate before, with all the excellent perks and privileges that had come with being born into rock royalty?

Now that he'd tasted such delicious emotion, could he ever go back to living without it again?

Duke straightened and unhooked the guitar strap. "You're all too kind. I'm taking thirty and then I'll be back— if I can wait that long. Please take the time to enjoy another drink and patronize the Casino Club, and to say something nice to the one you're with."

More applause sounded, and Duke appreciated it above and beyond the deafening cacophonies so routine during 3-D concerts because it was so honest. He started toward the dressing room, high on adrenaline, high on the music.

"Seamus?" asked a man's voice. "Seamus Whyler?"

It took the second mention of his alter ego's name before Duke realized the man was speaking to him. Duke revolved. "Yeah, bud?"

"*Bud,*" the man chuckled. "That's why I'm here. One of my buddies said you've been playing this joint. Figured I'd check it out for myself and see if it was true."

"A fan, I'm honored," Duke said. He extended his hand.

"Fan?" the man laughed again. "You don't remember me, do you, Whyler?"

The man shoved an envelope into Duke's outstretched hand.

"What's this?" Duke asked.

"How quickly you shit-bags forget. You rented an apartment from me three years ago, *bud*," the man said, his voice rising. "And you checked out, leaving me owed twelve hundred bucks. *This* is a demand, and if you don't pay up, I'm going to start getting loud out there, in front of your fans, you asshole."

Duke choked down a dry swallow. Twelve hundred bucks was nothing to him, the amount of money the band burned through at a restaurant in a single night. Only he wasn't with the band. He had maybe fifty bucks on him, another two hundred coming after the gig.

"Man, I'm so sorry," he started.

"You sure as fuck are, you fucking deadbeat."

Duke held up a hand. "I'm not like that. I want to pay you. I've got part of it on me." He reached for his wallet.

"Tell you what, scum-ball—you'd better find a way to land your greasy fingers on the rest of it pretty damn quick, because if you don't, I'll call the cops. I've wasted enough of my life trying to track you down. You either pay up *now* or else I'll see you in court."

The police? He couldn't risk the truth coming out.

The dude huffed out a disgusted sigh and turned, and Duke suffered another new emotion he'd never experienced before—the cold sweats over being flat broke, after some angry debtor's backed your spine up against a wall. His heart pounded in his ears and all the moisture drained from his mouth.

So this was what it meant to suffer for one's art.

"I'll pay you back, I swear," Duke promised.

He could see that an invisible wall had gone up in the time it took to ask the question. To ask for help. To beg for a loan, something Duke had never been forced to do before this night.

"I'm sure you're good for it," Toby said. He patted at his backside. "But I don't have my checkbook on me, just my wallet and credit cards. Let me sprint home and get it—one of the benefits of living so close to work, right?"

Toby smiled, but the gesture seemed to come through a filter. Money... Duke had always had it. He still did, just no easy access to his fortune. But he was Seamus now, and Seamus was flat broke, and this taste of walking in the man's shoes was bitter.

"I swear, I'm gonna pay you back."

"Don't worry, if you don't I'll take it out in trade," Toby said.

The two men hugged and that, on the outside, was the end of it. Only it didn't feel like the end to Duke. He was in debt to another human being, a strange and uncomfortable predicament he hadn't known since—

Since Jack Dalton, his dad. Until five or so years ago, he'd owed his dad everything, a fact the old man had loved to remind him of, usually when he was sauced.

Fifteen minutes later, Toby was back at the Casino Club with a check made out for twelve hundred dollars. Duke filled out the man's name—Adam Laraby, according to the demand for payment.

"Thanks," Duke said, wiping his brow.

"No sweat. You saved my ass from the fire tonight, so the least I could do is rescue yours."

THE DICK—ADAM Laraby—studied the check. "This thing bounces, I'm coming after you as well as him."

"It won't," Toby said.

Laraby exhaled loudly, a dismissive gesture meant to drive home his wrath. "We'll just see about that, first thing in the morning at your bank."

He shot Duke a look before exiting the club. Duke made it to the second set on time, but the energy he brought to the first half was gone, smothered by the crushing weight of reality as it related to the artist's life.

"It's been a long night. I'm gonna crash," Toby said.

"You do that. I'll be in shortly."

Toby nodded and waved. Duke tipped his chin in response and offered a weak smile. For the first time since cutting ties with the old man and laying down the gauntlet with his no-drinking rule, he could have gone for a beer. Hell, something stronger. There was alcohol in the cottage. Toby had beer and scotch and a bottle of chilly vodka in the freezer.

Only once he started, Duke knew he might not stop. Another thing he owed his dad.

"Fuck," Duke sighed.

He settled on the sofa and reached for the scrapbook. Luckily, right before the first set, he'd grabbed a coaster from the bar that bore the Casino Club's logo; otherwise, he would have forgotten following his encounter with Laraby, the miserable money-grubbing fuck. Seamus had owed the dude serious green, granted. Still, Duke had trouble finding any sympathy for the prick.

Sighing, he reached for the scrapbook, hoping Seamus's beloved talisman would dispel the shitty blanket of angst trying to smother him. He noticed the letter sticking out, the one from Wanda Cofield, opened it, and read.

Track 14

THE FIRST SHOT went down fast and hard. It had been so long since Seamus drank anything stronger than beer that he'd forgotten the burn that lit on his tongue, accelerated on the plunge down the throat and detonated in the gut. He wagged his finger and indicated another. The next drink hurt, too.

"Want me to start a tab?"

"Hell, yeah," Seamus said. "And while you're at it, leave the bottle."

The second show in San Francisco hadn't ended any better than the first, because he had yet again refused to whip out his dick and jerk it for the audience. He'd given them a few teasing lifts of the kilt, but that failed to stop the booing. The boos now echoed in his head, killing the memory of the applause. Seamus's skin wasn't nearly as thick as he believed; all those small clubs and shitty door cash deals had not prepared him for the tongue-lashing he'd received two nights running in a major U.S. city's biggest concert venue.

He wanted to crawl into a hole and die. In a way, he was and hoped the alcohol being pumped into his blood would surgically target the precise brain cells where the memory was housed, killing it forever. Seamus hadn't drunk like this in a long time, because going on a tear cost money, even low-shelf. He had money now, lots of it. He planned on burning more than a few bucks—and brain cells—tonight. Anything to be free of the booing; anything to not think about their next destination—the Pavilion in Portland, Oregon. Another packed house. Another angry mob ready to chop off his balls for not showing his dick.

Seamus's stomach twisted into knots, and he felt his gorge rise. Only the greatest effort kept all that top-shelf liquor from taking an encore. Something sour bubbled up his throat. Seamus tossed back his head and focused on the ceiling in an attempt to choke it down. The ceiling over the bar was mirrored. He faced his own reflection but wondered who was staring back.

For so long, he'd gazed into the rearview mirror and he'd known that face, the reflection that of a simple, passionate man, poor as a proverbial fucking pauper yet so rich in other ways. A man with one true love, his music. The rest didn't really matter, because they'd suffered together, he and the music, and they were still together despite all they'd been put through, still in love. As long as he had his guitar and his scrapbook and enough gas money to make it to the next destination, he'd be better than okay.

What had happened to that man? Seamus didn't know, couldn't remember. Because the face staring down from the ceiling of the first bar he'd found after fleeing the concert was that of a man who, by all rights, should have been beyond happy, beyond fucking euphoric, but wasn't. A man with buckets of money, a shitload of fame, a mansion, a fleet of vehicles, a private jet—

And Seamus would trade it all for the chance to be back in his car, the car that stank of a man's sweat and long, restless miles, with his guitar and scrapbook at the ready, unburdened by all the bullshit.

"Bullshit's right," Seamus grumbled, his stomach quieting enough for him to speak.

Bullshit, because when you got right down to it, this life wasn't really about the music. It was about theater, and the bloodshed demanded by hungry crowds dating all the way back to Ancient Rome. Thousands of so-called fans, and it was more important for them to watch him honk on his hog and squirt all over the front row than listen to the actual performance. And that performance had been spot-on. Better than that, he'd done an excellent job. He *was* a rock star, but that wasn't good enough. The crowd wanted a porn star!

Seamus slowly poured, watching the oily brown liquid fall into the glass, capturing the light. His ears recorded the guttural *glug* and the makings of a song's lyrics briefly formulated in his thoughts, a ghost there one instant, gone the next. He raised the glass to his lips and swallowed.

When was the last time a new song had tempted him to scramble for paper and pen? A week? A new record, he thought, feeling the guilt and something worse. Defeat? And it had come about late one night following practice, when he was lying in bed, thinking about Joe-Kev. Joe-Kev. So mysterious and silent, so handsome.

A shadow teased the corner of his eye as another body slid onto the unoccupied barstool beside him. Seamus turned, scowled.

"What the hell do you think you're doing?" Harley asked in that imperious, autocratic tone.

Seamus tried to remember the excellent head given in the limo and the tightness of the man's ass, which he'd enjoyed so often during the early days of this masquerade, but couldn't imagine entering now that they were in the thick of the game.

"What does it look like I'm doing?"

"Breaking the rules."

"Whose rules?" Seamus sighed before knocking back another. This time, the booze went down easier, which worried him more than when it had stung because that meant he was getting used to it. Numb. The booze was working its voodoo.

"Duke's rules," Harley said. "More to the point, the rules of the contract you signed. You have an obligation to do what you're being paid to, and a big part of that is not putting 3-D and Duke Dalton at risk through your behavior."

"You have a problem with me enjoying a bottle of decent scotch, but it's okay for me to go out there and swing my dick at the world?"

Harley swept the room with a nervous glance. "Lower your fucking voice. And let me remind you that you knew what you were in for at the start. Now let's get you back to the bus before this spirals out of control."

Seamus fixed Harley with a scowl. "No wonder he couldn't stand it and had to get out."

"Excuse me?"

"Duke," Seamus continued. "The dude obviously hasn't had a happy day—one truly, happy fucking day—his entire adult life. I wouldn't be surprised if, while he's grinding into that ass of yours, you tell him when he can come and how hard. You ever think about loosening up a little and just trying to enjoy the ride?"

"*This* is a business," Harley said coldly. "So fuck you, dude. You didn't seem to mind it when my mouth or my ass was making you come."

"Whatever," Seamus said, turning away.

Harley slid off the barstool. "That's great. Real sharp answer you got there."

"Fuck off."

"Maybe later, once the tour bus is moving and we're on our way." Harley reached into his pocket and pulled out three bills—a ten and two twenties. He tossed them onto the bar top. "Come on."

Seamus said, "Don't you pay my tab, and don't order me around. You don't own me, dude."

"No, but Duke does. If you don't walk out of here right now with me—while you're still able to walk—we're gonna have ourselves a real ugly problem, one you seriously won't appreciate."

Harley strutted away, confidence showing in his strides, his ass. Seamus finished what was left in his glass and tried—oh, how he tried—to focus on the bottle. But the ominous threat soon had his legs in motion, and he was following after those snakeskin boots, that ass, a trained puppy dog, a puppet.

Duke not only owned his body but also his soul and Seamus resented it. They'd cornered him, caged him, killed his muse.

The room spun and twice he nearly tripped on his way out of the bar to the waiting taxi.

THE TOUR BUS'S wheels glided over the pavement, creating a hypnotic song. *An elegy,* thought Seamus, who lay sprawled across one of the cushioned benches lining the table between the front of the bus and the bunks where the rest of the band snoozed. A funeral dirge. The melody of dead dreams and lost hope. It crossed his mind that someone should record this music and find a way to incorporate it into a Goth-rock song.

The alcohol souring in his system retaliated with a sickening lurch. Seamus was no lightweight, but the jolt hit him particularly hard and, while puking his guts into the toilet, he couldn't help but wonder how much of it was the scotch and how much owed to the cold reception he'd gotten upon his return to the tour bus, safely tethered to Harley's invisible leash. Two big geysers cleared out his stomach. His diaphragm hurt only half as much as his head, which began to pound worse following the expulsion. Thick, clotted tears filled his eyes. The snarky voice in Seamus's thoughts figured he wouldn't need Perry or his white face paint to pass for Duke De Morte for a while.

The reflection in the bathroom mirror while he brushed his teeth confirmed it. Seamus hadn't recently expired; this state of decomposition looked long past actual death.

The short march back to the common area was a miserable few steps that felt like staggering along the deck of a ship bouncing in hurricane seas. He briefly considered making it to the bunks, but the looks he'd gotten from Shaye and Arif were almost as grating as the headache pounding drumbeats into his gray matter. Joe-Kev hadn't been easy to read. Joe-Kev never was. Besides, he hadn't managed to force himself to meet the other man's gaze at the time. Sleep was a hopeful notion. Seamus's agony, however, was tangible.

He stretched out on the cushion but couldn't get comfortable. Then, the voice in his head asked why he expected to. This was the price you paid. Thinking about the scrapbook and the acoustic guitar only worsened the malady. So he listened to the music of the road, but not for very long.

Several replicated clones of Joe-Kev wavered in the corridor when Seamus peeled open his eyes, alerted to the soft scuffle of footsteps. It took a half dozen rapid blinks for the several Joe-Kevs to pull back into one. The one and only.

"Hey," Seamus said.

Joe-Kev nodded in greeting. "You okay?"

"That's up to interpretation," he answered, attempting humor.

Joe-Kev flashed the barest of smiles, so the attempt succeeded, at least partially.

"Hope I didn't wake you up with that carnival in the head."

"I wasn't really sleeping," Joe-Kev said. He hovered at the edge of the table, hands tucked into his pockets. The sleep drifting around him, messing with his overall image, was complimentary, creating a moment glimpsed through a different lens. "Mind if I crash up here with you?"

"Fuck no, of course not."

Seamus smiled, sat up fully, and scooted aside, making room. It suddenly dawned on him that his skull was pounding less, but his heart was in a hell of a gallop.

Joe-Kev sat next to him, stone-faced as usual, except for the knot in his throat as he choked down a swallow. A hint of his scent, that clean masculine sweat a real man's body exudes, seasoned Seamus's next breath. The pain inside him abated.

"Thanks for checking in," he said.

Joe-Kev said, "No worry, man. We've all been there."

"There?"

"Fucked up. Don't let anyone try to pull the wool over your eyes."

"Really? 'Cause it feels like I got a pair of angry sheep trampling on each eyeball."

Joe-Kev chuckled in response. It was the most the guy had said or emoted since they met on that naked morning, which now felt eons in the past.

"Dude, I know you're an asset to the band."

Seamus's next breath came with difficulty. "You do?"

Joe-Kev nodded. "If we didn't have you... you're not Duke, man."

Right as Seamus expected Joe-Kev to deliver some damning sentiment—*you're not as good*—the dude again surprised him.

"In many ways, you're better."

This brought them eye-to-eye. Neither man spoke after that for what seemed a very long time, for words weren't necessary.

"Wow, dude," Seamus sighed. "Better?"

"Sure. I've been on that stage dozens of times, dozens, when I could tell that Duke's heart wasn't in it. But you... even when we're only jamming, I can see how into it you are. You don't just feel the music; you *are* the music."

Seamus fell back into the pull of Joe-Kev's gaze. He couldn't remember wanting to be in another human being's company as much as now, or seeing anyone as so physically attractive, so sexually compelling. The hangover surrendered to his hard-on.

"Thanks, buddy," Seamus said while fighting the urge to flash one of those big, goofy grins.

"Welcome," Joe-Kev said, a hint of ruddy color rising on his throat. Then, in a lower voice, he added, "That whole not-drinking thing's a touchy subject, if you hadn't guessed."

"I had."

Joe-Kev leaned closer. The temperature inside the tour bus plummeted before surging up to a scorcher. "It's because of Duke's dad, Jack Dalton. During the Stage Fright years, he got into drinking, snorting, all of it."

Seamus tried to focus, which proved nearly impossible given the other man's closeness, his scent, his magnificence. "Yeah?"

"I don't want to betray Duke. Him and me..." Joe-Kev's voice trailed to a whisper before surging back. "We're good buddies, which is why I can say he's gone on stage in body, but not in soul. Duke suffered some ugly neglect whenever the old man got sauced."

"Shit."

"So you understand why?"

Seamus nodded. "Thanks, pal." He extended his hand. Joe-Kev met the offer with a knuckle-knock. "And it goes no further."

"I didn't think it would."

What happened next was unexpected—and more wonderful on the heels of so shitty a night than he could have expected. Joe-Kev asked him about his history, his music, his life. In the exchange, Seamus learned Joe-Kev was the youngest of three brothers, had been banging on drums since he was a boy, and had been married once, divorced, and there'd been no one else. Until Duke.

"What?" Seamus asked.

"It wasn't anything, not to him," Joe-Kev admitted, a dose of what Seamus assumed to be guilt causing the man's eyebrows to knit.

"If that's the case, the dude's a fool," Seamus sighed. "Because man, you're solid fucking gold."

Joe-Kev glanced nervously around. When it was clear that they were still alone, he bridged the distance and kissed Seamus on the cheek. The hot and itchy thickness between his legs complained by pushing against his zipper. Seamus adjusted his cock and, as Joe-Kev pulled away, he reached his other hand out, cupped his neck, and drew the man back. Their next kiss was full on the lips, and the best of Seamus's life.

The taste of Joe-Kev's mouth was better than top-shelf booze, better than all the mouths that came before it.

"Dude," Joe-Kev said, breaking the kiss. "You have no idea how much I've wanted this. Wanted *you*. But before we get too crazy, there's something I gotta tell you."

"Sure, what is it?"

"I think you should do it, in Portland."

THE SILKY-SMOOTH instrumental began. Duke De Morte made his circle around the band members, orbited back to his position, and right as the boos started, he lifted his kilt and wagged his hard, glowing cock at the crowd.

Seamus jerked off for the Portland audience. The boos turned to cheers. And somewhere in the third row, center, one camera, in particular, recorded the performance in exacting detail.

Track 15

DUKE REREAD THE letter.

The muted crash of the waves filtering through the open window added a layer of melancholy to the words. Words in which Wanda Cofield poured out her heart to Seamus, telling him how much she loved him, but knowing it wasn't going to work because he would always love his music more. She understood that, she claimed. But she had chosen to walk away rather than live in his first love's shadow.

In the wake of reaching the final line, coldness blanketed him. Compounding Duke's malaise was the lingering fallout of that night at the Casino Club. The debt was Seamus's, really, only Duke had claimed ownership. No amount of plucking on the guitar helped. As the morning dragged on, it became clear that the melancholy would only deepen the longer he stayed trapped inside the cottage with it.

A warm summer drizzle pissed over the day, so a walk along the beach wasn't the best choice for escape. Duke grabbed the letter and the keys to Seamus's car. A drive was what he needed. And he was fairly sure of where he was headed, even if he didn't admit it when he called Toby.

"Hey, I'm heading out. Just need to clear my head. Where? North, should be back later. Yeah, back at you, babe."

He drove away from Bay Breeze and the beach and headed up Route 117, traveling old school. In his former life,

Duke was chauffeured everywhere he went, except when he took one of the cars in his fleet out for a drive. His GPS navigation system always accompanied him. Now, as Seamus Whyler, he'd picked up a map at a gas station.

A sign for Winter Woods appeared at the side of the road. Duke's heart began to race. He didn't know why he was here or what he'd do once he reached the address on the envelope.

The house sat in a tree-lined neighborhood of single-family homes. One story, the gray paint was chipped and fading in spots, and the paved driveway showed cracks. From the road, you could tell the yard needed some help, only there was never enough spare time in the day for the people who lived there to pick up fallen branches or to keep the lawn in a perfect green buzz cut.

He drove slowly past the house, circled at the corner, and drove back. By then the drizzle had died and a humid mist floated over the afternoon. Through the haze, Duke saw that the name on the mailbox read, *Cofield*.

There was no garage, the driveway empty. Duke pulled over to the curb and let the car idle. So this was the life his alter ego had renounced for one spent living as a wandering minstrel, playing his guitar and sleeping behind the wheel. The earlier sense of melancholy returned, only stronger. He had no way of knowing if this was a house where music lived and songs were sung, but its exterior seemed to telegraph a different mindset. Maybe that's why Seamus let her go, Duke thought.

Images of his own life formed in his mind's eye then began to spiral, unspool. Until the switch, he'd never experienced being in love. Love of music. Love of another human being. The availability of sex and stardom had occluded those passions. According to Duke's research, this woman was the second love of Seamus's life.

Duke had fallen in love with music, and with Toby. If forced to make a similar choice, would he pick one over the other? Was it possible to love both man and muse, in equal doses? These questions veiled his biggest concern, which was what would happen after the Death Heart 2 Tour was over, and Duke was faced with returning to his real life? How would Toby—and the music—fit in there?

Maybe they wouldn't.

Duke sighed and pinched the corners of his eyes. Maybe these new loves of his weren't real, simply illusions, dreams. And as with all dreams, waking up was inevitable.

A knock sounded on the window, jarring Duke out of his inner monologue. Standing on the other side of the foggy glass was an older woman. A mutt tugged on the leash in her grasp.

Duke rolled down the window. "Hey."

"Can I help you?" she asked. The question seemed genuine, not a demand.

"I'm looking for Wanda," he answered before he could assess the statement, right or wrong.

"Are you family?"

"Yes."

"She's probably still at work. You know the place?"

Duke shook his head. "Afraid not."

"It's the little diner across from the Falls. Downtown. Dewey Decibels."

Duke grinned. "Cute."

"You can't miss it."

"I'll try not to. Thanks."

Duke rolled up the window and pulled onto the road. He turned toward town. Before long, he was traveling down a hill, between a stretch of brick buildings on his right and a collection of white New England houses to the left whose lower levels had been converted to the kinds of cottage businesses one would expect to find in a small town with a charming name like Winter Woods—a quilt shop, a stationery store, a parlor that served homemade ice cream, a pottery shop. He glanced again to his right in time to see the wall of red brick end. Beyond, a waterfall tumbled and ran beneath the road, which became bridge. Back to his left, on the corner beside a small park and gazebo on the bank of the water, sat another two-story house, white. The lower level bore a colorful sign that proclaimed: The Dewey Decibel Diner.

He found a parallel parking spot farther up the road and backtracked to the diner's front door. There, a sandwich board advertized the day's specials—a cold summer fruit soup, roasted red pepper and ham panini, and scallop scampi. All of it sounded great. Duke's mouth watered and his stomach grumbled in response. The last thing he'd eaten was a peanut butter sandwich on two English muffins, some nine hours earlier, with coffee.

Duke reached the door only to stop and redirect his hand. He'd gassed up just outside of Bay Breeze. The tank had taken forty bucks, and that had only filled it to the three-quarter mark. He only had ten left to his name. These days ten bucks didn't get a man very far, even in a diner.

Duke's stomach complained again, this time owing to nerves more than hunger.

Part diner and part used bookstore, the rest of the limited space inside the Dewey Decibel Diner was devoted to music. Used vinyl and cassettes, some CDs, even secondhand musical instruments were for sale. On the public notice board, a schedule of events listed performers who were set to play in a corner of the diner. A poetry open mike, the acoustic stylings of a guy who'd once jammed with the Doobie Brothers, and local legend and coffee slinger Wanda Cofield were all part of the week's upcoming highlights.

A dozen tables and booths occupied the right front of the diner. Books in the middle and left, in front of the kitchen, and music to the right rear, where an upright piano defined the space. A trio of antique Underwood typewriters was fixed to the wall as three-dimensional artwork. Watercolors and oils, even one painting on black velvet, decorated the rest. All of it worked well.

If Wanda Cofield was working the shift, Duke didn't see her. He scooted past the dining section, which was half full of customers, and into the used records. The smell of fried food—French fries and fish, mushrooms and mozzarella—twisted his guts into knots. Had he ever been this hungry? While flipping through records, he accessed a memory, not a pleasant one, of being on the road with his dad. They were on the East Coast, he remembered, in a club. A private club. The old man was drinking. Jack Dalton's kid was only allowed in because, well, he was Jack Dalton's kid. They offered him a cold soda, but in all the excitement and theater, Jack had forgotten to feed Duke, who was only six or seven in this particular memory. An entire day without eating.

Hell, Duke thought, there were kids in Third World countries that were lucky to eat once every three, but at the time it had seemed like the worst fate imaginable.

"I'm starving, dad," whispered a voice in Duke's thoughts. His voice, only a version two decades removed.

"Let me just finish this one drink and I'll order you some dinner."

Only it hadn't ended at one drink, and no dinner came. It was lunch the next day before Duke's sobs roused his father out of his stupor.

The memory punched him in the stomach. There were so many others, many of them worse.

Last he knew, the old man was dying. Of course, Jack Dalton had been dying for a decade. Duke clamped down on the thoughts and ceased window-shopping. A telephone rang behind the register.

"Triple-D," a woman's voice said. "Yup, this is the diner."

Duke spun around. He hadn't made the connection until that moment—the Dewey Decibel Diner. Triple-D. The nickname made sense, but the serendipity of the coincidence launched a shiver down his spine. Duke Donovan Dalton. 3-D.

The woman on the phone jotting down what he assumed to be a takeout order was blonde, beautiful. It was Wanda Cofield. A second ghost walked over Duke's grave. Seamus's grave, the voice in his head corrected. Even so, Duke turned around, giving her his back, and vanished into the used book section, until the coast was clear. From the cut of his eye, he watched her dip into the kitchen. Duke turned and marched toward the door.

He almost made it out of the diner without being spotted.

"Seamus?" Wanda called.

Clearly, her visit to the kitchen had been a short one. Duke kept walking.

"Seamus Whyler?"

Duke froze with one hand on the door. What had he been thinking in coming here? Maybe he wasn't, not clearly. He turned, and the look on her face was one of complete shock.

"Oh my God."

Duke choked down a dry swallow. "Hello, Wanda."

"What are you doing here?"

Duke said the first thing that came to mind. "Having lunch."

He ordered the safest, most-reasonable thing on the menu—a club sandwich and fries, with soda. Until the food arrived, conversation had been sparse.

Wanda set the plate down, just hard enough to relay her unhappiness. She took the seat across from him without being asked. "Why are you here, Seamus?"

"I wanted to see you."

"What for?"

"Uh... to see you. Make sure you're okay."

"I was up until about fifteen minutes ago. So talk."

"Before I do, you didn't spit on my food, did you?"

"No, but that doesn't mean I didn't do worse."

Duke pushed the plate away.

"Oh, don't be so ridiculous. You know I didn't."

Duke did not, but he took her at her word. "I was only curious. I didn't come here to stir up anything. I'm not here to cause trouble."

Wanda's eyes drilled into him. "Good. You look well. A little different."

"You look great."

She huffed a humorless laugh and left the check, print side down, beside the plate. "Enjoy your meal. You need anything else, be quick. I'm almost done here."

"You're performing tonight?"

"No, tomorrow. Too bad you won't be here."

She stood and walked briskly away. Duke ate the sandwich, which was delicious, but the experience crashed completely when he flipped over the bill. In placing his order under Wanda's scrutiny, he hadn't factored in the tax or the tip. Nine bucks and thirty-three cents, minus gratuity.

"Shit," he grumbled.

So far, the reunion hadn't gone much better for Duke than the original relationship for Seamus. He grabbed the bill and a pen from the counter and scribbled hastily across the top.

He caught Wanda right as she was exiting the kitchen with her tote in hand, her shift concluded.

"Wanda," he said.

Lips pursed, she studied him, and he could tell that at the edge of the woman's anger was a note of desire. "What?"

Duke handed her the slip and the ten.

"What's this?"

In a lower voice, Duke said, "I only have a ten on me. I'm light on the tip."

Wanda's eyes narrowed as she read the scribble on the receipt. "What the hell is this—an I.O.U.? Are you serious?"

"Afraid so."

"Same old Seamus," she said, sighing. "Still writing checks I'll never be able to cash. Forget it."

"Wanda, please."

"*I.O.U.—a huge tip, name it, it's yours*? How about this, Seamus—never, ever come back here again. Don't darken my doorstep or waste my time or screw with my bliss? How's that for you?"

She tossed the money and the slip into the register before walking away, leaving Duke standing alone beneath the scrutiny of those eating their meals close enough to hear the exchange.

Duke thought about driving home. *Home.* Funny how the beach cottage and Toby now felt more like home than the compound and studio in California. He looked back up the hill and turned toward Bay Breeze, but got only as far as

Wanda's neighborhood. Right as the drizzle returned, he found himself parking along the street in front of the house. What he assumed was Wanda's car now sat in the driveway. Lights were on inside. Duke debated leaving again but for the second time talked himself into staying.

He couldn't leave, not like this. Not after fucking things up potentially for Seamus and definitely for Wanda. He exited the car. The drizzle up-tempoed into a warm, unpleasant summer rain that stuck to the skin. The humidity had risen, too, worsening the effect. He made it to the front door, cleared his throat, knocked.

The door opened. Duke glanced down. A boy no more than six years old stood on the other side. With his dark hair and emerald gemstone eyes, he was the spitting image of a young Duke, who once went hungry while his old man got polluted. More to the point, the boy was also a younger version to Duke's reflection, Seamus.

"Hi," the boy said.

"Hi," Duke answered.

From inside the house, Wanda called, "Angus, who's at the door?"

The boy turned and ran away. "Mommy, it's a man."

A scuffle of hasty footsteps sounded. Wanda appeared, and her parting look of frustration at the diner paled to that which now crossed her face.

"No," she said. "You can't be here. You *can't*."

Then tears began to spill down Wanda's cheeks, and she howled something terrible. Duke reached for her, intending only to comfort. Without warning, she started to hit, to struggle, the attack so violent, at first Duke didn't realize the boy was kicking and punching and yelling, too.

"Leave my mommy alone!" Angus shouted.

Wanda ceased struggling at the sound of her son's voice and her tears stemmed. She pulled the boy into her arms and Duke caught the angry, confused glare, not knowing what to say or daring to speak.

Eventually, Wanda leaned her lips toward his ear and whispered, "Not in front of Angus."

Duke nodded.

What felt like hours later, while he sat on her sofa and the boy was finally asleep, she confessed.

"You shouldn't be here, Seamus. There's nothing here for you, no reason for you to be in this house. No reason for you to stay."

Duke shrugged. He needed to know. Not for himself, but for Seamus's sake. "Is he...?"

"Yours? He's mine, and he's a great kid. That's all you need to know. We're okay. We're a hundred and ten percent fine."

Duke glanced around the living room. It was, as she said, a fine life by all outward signs. Cozy and colorful, a home where a single mom had raised her son to the best of her ability. And Wanda's best, obviously, was better than most.

"Why didn't you tell me?"

"For the same reason I'm not going to tell him," she said, indicating the direction of Angus's room, where a constellation of glow-in-the-dark stars shimmered on the ceiling. "There's no reason to. You dare come back and make demands after all this time? You already walked away."

Duke glanced at his glass of soda on the coffee table, half-empty, perspiring as the ice cubes melted from squares to circles. The scene was a moment frozen in time that he would never forget, an ugly secret, a lie that would burden him for the rest of his days.

The cell phone rang. Seamus's phone. Duke grabbed it.

"Hey, man," Toby said.

"Hey."

"You on your way home?"

"Soon," Duke said. But that, too, was a lie.

Track 16

IT WAS JUST the two of them. Two men and the music, ignoring the rows of designer guitars and all the other trappings of wealth and fame. Seamus handled a cheap acoustic guitar he'd paid to have delivered from a used instrument store on Hollywood Boulevard—the fee to have it brought to the gate twice what the beat-up guitar cost. Horribly out of tune, he'd worked it back into shape. Two men and the music. Two men and *their* music.

Bare-chested, barefoot, Joe-Kev sat at the drums, looking like a force of nature. Sounding like one, too. His hands unleashed thunder, and Seamus's heart pulsed in response. So did his dick. One was as important as the other, he agreed, while plucking at the strings, lost in the music. Lost in Joe-Kev.

The swing through three cities—including Austin, the original scene of the crime that had launched 3-D past the stratosphere—had gone mostly without incident. Whatever waltz he and Joe-Kev had done around one another for the weeks leading up to the long, laborious bus ride had become a private slow-dance, more satisfying and wonderful than anything Seamus had known before. Their impromptu rendition of George Benson's brilliant "On Broadway" carried in the air elegantly, sensual in its delivery. The undercurrent of sex and sweat, lingering from that afternoon's first cycle of lovemaking, embossed the words and the beats. Seamus's cock pulsed in a pair of Duke's loose-fitting cotton shorts. The guitar thrummed in concert, like an extension of his hardness.

Seamus crooned. His eyes met Joe-Kev's, and the surge of emotion was so intense that Seamus forgot the next line. What emerged was gobbledygook, still playful in their private setting.

Joe-Kev ceased hammering thunder-beats and choked up laughing. As had happened so often during the past few days, he jumped up, marched over, and started to play on Seamus's back with his drumsticks. Seamus stood up from the stool. Joe-Kev drummed on his ass.

"Stop it," Seamus chuckled.

"No," Joe-Kev said.

Seamus unhooked the guitar and set it down. Turning, he came face to face with Joe-Kev, and all it took was a glance into those amazing blue eyes to forget everything he intended to say.

Joe-Kev gave his nipples a follow-up; the drumsticks conducted electricity through the flimsy cover of Seamus's T-shirt.

"Very funny."

Joe-Kev's eyes narrowed. "Very sexy."

Seamus cupped the cleanly clipped back of Joe-Kev's head. "Yes, you sure are, dude."

He drew Joe-Kev closer. Their lips met in a firm kiss. Seamus initiated deeper contact with his tongue. Joe-Kev opened, taking him in. The taste of their earlier tango on the sofa in the studio's lounge area ignited on the next kiss. Seamus reached down, intending to free his cock, but Joe-Kev's hand got there first. Seamus moaned into the other man's mouth. Joe-Kev grunted in response.

He'd sucked Seamus on the bus, and Seamus had returned the affection. The road between Oregon, Seattle, Las Vegas, and Austin, the halfway point on the six-week, ten-city tour, had been a continuing exploration of unexpected discovery. As Joe-Kev freed Seamus from his shorts and Seamus savored the taste of Joe-Kev's tongue, the irony again struck home, that of a couple of hairy, athletic he-men gone mad over one another. The defining line between dominant and submissive, Top and Bottom, didn't exist. They were a pair of Yangs minus a Yin. And still, it worked.

Better than Seamus thought possible.

"You're magnificent, dude," he whispered.

"Whatever," Joe-Kev said lightly. Then he dropped to his knees on the expensive designer carpet, and Seamus's cock vanished down Joe-Kev's throat. The pressure drove him to the tops of his bare toes, better than anything he'd ever experienced. *Ever*, including his days with Wanda, his brief time with Toby, even that double-dicked circus act he and Duke had pulled on Harley's ass, which previously held top bragging rights.

Joe-Kev took him almost to the balls, an action that launched shivers into rippling through his flesh. When the sensation passed and he was able to see again, it was Joe-Kev before him, no one else.

Love. Who'd have guessed?

Seamus dropped. Wordlessly, he stripped off Joe-Kev's shorts and the gray boxer briefs beneath, exposing the incredible cock he'd grown to know intimately, in every detail. The skull tattooed across the top of its shaft stretched out; instead of a symbol of death, Seamus saw only new life because he was certain that no matter what happened in the days ahead, there would always be a place for Joe-Kev in them. There had to be.

Seamus wiggled fully out of his shorts and tugged the T-shirt over his shoulders. He grabbed Joe-Kev's face and kissed him hard on the lips before assuming the same comfortable position he'd grown to love since returning to Dymond Encerito, a pair of Yangs, male Chinese symbols of light and heat and desert, sixty-nining on the floor of Duke Dalton's private recording studio.

The air smelled clean and rich; of Joe-Kev's skin, even better, of masculine sweat and the manly soap he'd bathed with that morning. Seamus caressed a length of calf muscle, the as-yet un-inked one, loving the scrape of leg hair between his fingers. He played with Joe-Kev's toes before sweeping his fingers back up, past the knee, and didn't stop until he was tugging on the man's meaty balls.

Seamus gave them a roll over his nostrils. The musky odor spurred him on. Sucking, he savored Joe-Kev's taste, magnified by the incredible feel of his lips around Seamus's cock. He imagined them forming a circle, creating a circuit. Two men, similar in body type and build, in rugged machismo. Similar in soul.

It was easy to feel so smitten when making love consisted of effortless times together, and always included the music.

Since the night on the bus, Seamus had written seven new songs. Five of them were worth being produced. Two, he knew, were solid gold. All of them owed to Joe-Kev and the connection they'd made.

Joe-Kev's tongue brushed Seamus's balls, and the world lurched out of its perfect orbit into something spiral, upside down. Seamus grunted a swear around Joe-Kev's thickness. Everything he'd learned about his soul mate made perfect sense—divorced, only to have a spark go off one night in the tour bus, with Duke. That factoid could have dampened Seamus's euphoria, only he now knew he wasn't merely a substitute for the band's lead singer. Joe-Kev had proven it was Seamus he loved, not Duke.

Smiling, Seamus stretched out. His cock pulsed in Joe-Kev's hand as he waited for the inevitable connection between Joe-Kev's tongue and his asshole. The anticipation was almost as maddening as the wet brush across his most sensitive flesh. He thought about the two of them in bed, him playing the guitar, Joe-Kev playfully tapping out a counterpoint rhythm on a bare length of leg, and his smile around the cock in his mouth widened. Had he ever felt this inspired? The voice in his thoughts answered with a damning follow-up question.

Would he ever feel this inspired again after the second Death Heart tour ended, and the next chapter of Seamus Whyler's life began?

The words and melody of a song covered by both George Benson and the Carpenters began to play in his thoughts, a favorite of Wanda's during the day. It tried to challenge his happiness as Joe-Kev ate his asshole with the enthusiasm of a starving man, and he sucked on his soul mate's tattooed cock.

When you got right down to it, Seamus *was* lost in a masquerade.

He willed the song to end, to be replaced by anything else, any other artist's lyric. For a brief and miserable moment, he heard the tune in Wanda's voice. The cruelty! Joe-Kev's tongue ran in a clockwise circle then reversed course, going counter before taking an up and down, side to side track. He only wanted to enjoy this moment, with this man.

Fuck, Seamus thought.

He ignored the lyrics the best that he could, and they both ignored the cadence of knocks on the locked studio door as long as possible. Seamus repeated the curse out loud as he pulled away from Joe-Kev's tongue and reached for his clothes. Joe-Kev grabbed his and ducked out of sight while Seamus answered the door.

He opened it angrily, partially. Harley stood on the other side, grim-faced, which wasn't a rarity these days.

"I told you we weren't to be disturbed," Seamus snapped.

Harley's eyes wandered around the silhouette of his body. The sweat on his face and the musty stink of two athletic men engaged in sex telegraphed his guilt, he thought, while Harley's eyes interrogated him. Little escaped that gaze.

"It couldn't be helped. We have an emergency. I need you up at the house for a meeting with the band. You and Joe-Kev, who I assume is out here with you. Practicing, was it?"

"Yeah, we were. Cut the bullshit. What's up, Harley?"

"There's a situation. The main house, if you can find the time to grace the rest of us with your presence."

Seamus sighed and tipped a glance over his shoulder to see Joe-Kev was back in his clothes, his erection tenting at the front of his shorts.

"You heard the little bitch," Seamus said, making sure to be loud enough so that Harley heard, too.

The two men marched out of the studio and up to the main house, where disaster awaited.

Shaye Floden was wearing less than Joe-Kev, only a pair of designer tight-whites and a thick gold chain. Arif sat in a sprawl in one of the big sofas, his spread legs in striped acid wash jeans, his feet in sandals, a white tank top and shades rounding out his wardrobe choice for the day. The dark expressions on the guitarist's and keyboard player's faces were impossible to misread.

"So who died?" Seamus grumbled.

"Maybe 3-D," Harley said. He crossed to the other side of the sofa, where his laptop sat open. A half-spin in Seamus's direction, and there it was, the damning news, spelled out clearly.

"Duke's Dick—or is this De Morte a different dude?" the headline posed. Accompanying the text were several pictures. The one at the top left, taken in Austin, was a close-up of the real Duke Dalton's cock, standing stiff between strokes. The one beside it on the right was clearly Seamus's, the wreath of foreskin around its head standing raised in the white makeup. Both cocks were a decent match save for that one obvious difference.

"I don't see the problem," Seamus said.

"Of course you don't, dickhead," Shaye chimed in. "You wouldn't see a bus coming at you in the middle of the street."

"Fuck you, Shaye."

"No, fuck *you*, Shame-boy."

Harley whistled a loud, sharp ceasefire. "Would you two dinkweeds cut the cock-knocking contest? This is serious enough without you boneheads whipping out the rulers. This isn't just any shitty blog, you know—it's Marquise Stilton's celebrity skin rag which, much as I hate to admit it, is about the biggest deal out there on the Web. This story's already been Chitted, FaceSpaced, and pirated by a thousand other, shittier blogs. By the end of this discussion, they'll be speculating about why Duke De Morte suddenly grew foreskin as far away as the Andromeda Galaxy. My phone's been ringing nonstop. All the publicists and pissants we've been denying access to the band since the last tour are now demanding answers. This is either going to be a public relations nightmare—"

"Or another fucking bonanza for the band," Seamus said. "Can you imagine how crazy the fans are going to be once we start our East Coast swing? You thought record downloads skyrocketed the last time? Imagine what this latest mystery will do for 3-D."

Arif sighed. "What the hell do you mean?"

"Think about it. Duke De Morte goes quiet after staging one of the wildest shows in live concert history. He returns from the dead six months later, and the biggest question isn't the how or the why, but *if*. If he'll whip out his dick and where, at which venue? You don't think that all the millions of diehards all over the planet won't eat this up, too? They're going to hang on and hold their breath, buy the T-shirts, the songs, and fuck their brains out dreaming of Duke's dick—and mine. Tell them nothing. It'll only make the whole sordid mess an even huger success!"

Arif and Seamus exchanged a look, and then Arif turned to Shaye, whose cock hung thick and obvious in the front of his underwear.

"What the fuck," Arif spat, throwing up his hands. "This whole scene's turned into one swinging dick after another. It's like a fucking sausage-fest around here lately. First, it was Duke... *Duke*, and we don't even know if we're ever going to see the dude again. And then *you*." This was meant for Seamus. "You, getting into a masturbating contest with this fucker." Arif nudged Shaye's thigh with the bottom of his sandal. "And now, our drummer."

Joe-Kev folded his arms. "What about me?"

"That's a great question," Shaye said. "What's up with the two of you dudes? Lately, you're like joined at the fucking hips. Or is it the ball sac? 'Cause it sure smells like a couple of ripe ones whenever I'm close to one of you."

"What's up," Joe-Kev answered matter-of-factly, "is that he's my buddy. Best friend I've ever had. Which is a hell of a lot more than you've ever offered to me. Any more questions, Shaye?"

As Seamus watched, admiring the dude's balls and loving his words, Joe-Kev stepped closer, and Shaye shrank from the imposing display of muscles.

"No, none," Shaye said. Even his cock looked less impressive in the wake of the surrender.

"So, do what you're so good at, Harley," Seamus said. "*Assist*. Ignore the problem, until it really becomes one."

"What I'm going to do is double our security. I don't care what Duke said—for the rest of this tour, you need to keep *that* hidden in your kilt, under wrap. And in your pants," Harley said, aiming a finger at Seamus's crotch.

It didn't matter how big the house was; in the days that followed, Harley moved Arif, Shaye, and Joe-Kev into three of the guest bedrooms, and the closed ranks felt more like a prison sentence during practice time. Trying to find privacy proved nearly impossible and, on several occasions, paparazzi or fans camped outside the main gate tried to scale the fence.

During the latest incident, which necessitated calling in the cops to escort the interlopers from the property, Duke's cell phone rang. Seamus didn't recognize the number on the caller I.D. It came up as Sperm Donor. He let it go to voicemail.

At the end of the excitement, he remembered the call and guessed who'd left the message, even as he played it.

"Duke, this is Jack... you know, your dad. Hey, I'm sure you don't want me calling, but... I've been hearing some crazy rumors, just wanted to make sure that you're okay. Wish you'd pick up or call me back. You know, maybe you

don't, but it's been three years now. Stone sober. No more of that shit. I wish you'd give me a little credit. I'm trying. Anyway, would you just give me a call, let me know you're all right? Please?"

Seamus started to hit the delete button. He played the message again, and his stomach tightened into knots. He knew one side of the story, but not the other. Still, the old man's plea was heartbreaking.

Later that night, thinking it the right thing to do, Seamus dialed Jack Dalton's number.

Track 17

"I DON'T WANT Angus to see you," Wanda said. "You have to promise me you'll be out of here before he gets up."

Duke promised he would. Wanda stood at the door to what he assumed was her bedroom dressed only in a camisole and a pair of silk shorts, short ones that showed her long, shapely legs. She hesitated and Duke's gaze lingered. She was a beautiful woman and he could tell, quite clearly, what Seamus had once seen in her. But around her beauty hung an aura of sadness, and you didn't have to be a rocket scientist, brain surgeon, or metrosexual in touch with his feminine side to recognize it.

Duke kicked off Seamus's well-traveled shoes and stretched out on the sofa. A borrowed pillow and blanket and the alien sounds of a stranger's house drove home the reality of couch surfing, that standard method of survival among so many hungry musicians. *Most* music makers, the voice in his thoughts reminded. Only those lucky enough to see their stars rise—or to be born into a life of stardom— avoided this particular rite of passage.

As he stretched out, feeling sweaty and uncomfortable, aware of a lump beneath his spine, he recalled part of an interview with Sheryl Crow, who'd said that her overnight success took fifteen long, hard years.

Maybe couch-surfing between gigs wasn't all that bad a deal, in reality, because it made you appreciate having an actual bed, especially when there was somebody wonderful beside you upon that hypothetical mattress. Maybe it also made you aware of your other blessings, like the art you were paying your dues and suffering for. In recent weeks, Duke had come to realize that expensive toys and wide-screen plasma televisions in high-def weren't what that life was all about. Life was having a quiet dinner with a great guy who'd not only blow you and lick your toes afterward, but who'd make you feel welcome in his bed and at his breakfast table for coffee and eggs the following morning. A garage loaded with cars so vintage you were lucky to drive them once in your lifetime between playing cities on a tour, no more than that out of fear of scratching the paint, couldn't compare to driving a shitty second-hand car on fumes to your next gig. You hoped you wouldn't run out of gas but knowing that if you did, you'd walk. Fuck, you'd crawl. Because even if only a dozen people waited, you were going to play your guitar and sing your best for them.

Life was not about high-end hotel suites and an endless parade of nameless, faceless holes to fuck or the illusion that they would ever be enough for you; life *was* about love, and love songs, and, yes, fucking—and knowing the other person's name and him knowing yours.

"*Toby*," Duke whispered.

The malaise hanging around him like the summer humidity intensified.

On Seamus's shitty little phone, which didn't take photos, shoot videos, or allow you to check e-mails, sports scores, or watch movies but was Duke's only lifeline to the outside world, he'd dialed Toby from Wanda's bathroom, gotten voicemail, and left a message stating he wouldn't be coming home that night. He'd be back tomorrow, probably late. When he'd told Wanda that he'd be spending the night in his car, because that's where he slept lately, she'd cast a look his way filled with regret for what had been, but more so for what now was. This new reality was a burden she didn't need. He could take the couch, but he'd have to be out before Angus woke up. She didn't want them being together, hanging out. Just forget that idea, dammit. Forget you were here, forget all that you saw and think you now know—about you, me, and especially Angus. The sofa, and nothing else.

Duke didn't fall asleep. Instead, he tossed and turned, sweated, told himself he should get up and drive, just drive back to Toby, to Toby's bed and Toby's morning coffee. Then he got hard, pulled out his cock, and milked a load into a sock. Ashamed, he wondered if that was an acceptable part of couch-surfing decorum, or if he'd broken some sacred rule. Once you jerked your dick on a fellow musician's couch, did you get booted off it permanently, meaning there was one less place to crash in the sofa network?

At just shy of five in the morning, Duke climbed off the couch and crept to the bathroom. He ran the shower lukewarm, stripped, and stepped in, not knowing if he'd remembered to bring a change of clothes on his mission of discovery to Winter Woods. Too late now, he stepped into the spray, desperately needing the shower even if it meant pulling on the same clothes bunched on the bathroom floor.

The shower's bath buddy was filled with a woman's shampoos and conditioners, floral soap, and body wash. Duke scrubbed and lathered, shampooed and rinsed. The scents of Wanda were exotic and arousing, though also bittersweet. But even this emotion was strangely exhilarating; anything that blew away the stagnancy he'd lived too much of his life in was a welcome change.

Duke stepped out and toweled dry. His socks and underwear were too fragrant to wear another day. The same held true for the shirt. Duke pulled on his jeans commando.

Bunching the rest of his clothes into a ball and carrying it like a football, he padded barefoot and bare-chested back into the hallway and nearly collided with Wanda.

"Seamus," she gasped.

Duke straightened. The truth came close to his lips, but not past them. He wasn't Seamus, not really, just a dude who looked so much like him it was uncanny. Admitting that to her, however, would manifest even bigger problems than the ones already there.

"I thought you were Angus," she said.

Duke shrugged. "Sorry, I tried to be quiet."

He forced a smile. She blocked his way. Duke started to move around her, but Wanda was again there in front of him, looking so fine in her satin shorts. Duke saw that her nipples stood out stiffly behind that flimsy layer of cotton. As their awkward dance continued, each moving out of the other's way at the same time only to wind up blocking any chance for escape, he caught a hint of her scent and knew she was aroused.

They ceased dancing. Wanda's trembling lips opened and she spoke Seamus's name once more, breathlessly, as if it were an incantation.

Then she reached for him and wrapped an arm around his neck. Duke fumbled the football-shaped bunch of dirty clothes and cupped the sides of her beautiful face. Their lips met; a blinding starburst of lust rolled over Duke and, for a brief, insane instant, all he could think about was fucking Wanda.

Her fingers walked over the tent in his pants, and sanity resumed. Duke broke the lip lock and seized Wanda's wrists.

"No," he said.

Wanda pressed the point. "Yes, Seamus."

Toby's face manifested in Duke's thoughts as a sense of betrayal and guilt socked him in the stomach. So this was what love felt like? True love, the kind of intense emotion that stops a man from fucking around, even when his dick wants to.

"I can't, Wanda," he said. "I'm not the man I used to be. I'm not the guy you once knew, the one who hurt you."

"Are you kidding?" she snapped.

Duke caressed her face. "You... you're so fucking hot, girl. But you know this is a mistake."

Wanda leaned into his touch, eyes half-closed, and whispered, "Please."

Duke shook his head. Wanda pulled away and turned around, giving him her back.

He reached for her. "Wanda..."

She shrugged out of his reach. "I can't believe I'm back here again, right where I was the last time you decided I wasn't good enough to be a factor in your world."

"Wanda, it's not like that."

"It isn't? I think you're right, Seamus. It was a mistake. So why don't you forget all about that I.O.U. and the sex we almost just had and, especially, forget about me and Angus."

"Don't—"

She spun around. "Don't *what*? Get out, now."

When he didn't move quickly enough, she shouted her demand again, and Duke honored it.

He found a fresh pair of socks and a T-shirt with the logo of a band he'd never heard of in the trunk and pulled them on. The morning was another soaker, and the gloomy atmosphere worsened the ache in the pit of Duke's stomach. Like crashing on the couch, Duke now knew what it was like to go hungry. He found a few bits of change on the floor of the car, but it didn't add up enough for a cup of coffee. There would be coffee back in Bay Breeze. Coffee, and so much more. Duke dialed Toby, only again the message went to voicemail.

Hungry and haggard, he thought about driving, only he really needed to be there at the Triple-D when she played. He needed to listen, not sure why, only convinced that he must.

Duke's stomach burbled. He had never experienced that level of misery since the long-ago day with Jack at the private club. Two full decades had passed, and still, the body hadn't forgotten the horror of being denied sustenance.

He spent much of the day in the car, flipping through Seamus's scrapbook. He plucked at the guitar. Mostly, he moped, closed his eyes, and felt lost. It wasn't until the day started to darken that he realized this, too, was one of the usual rites of passage for most musicians. Most other creative people, too.

Duke started the car and drove back into town. He found a parking spot and, nauseated from hunger and nervous for good reason, he entered the Dewey Decibel Diner.

He sat in a dark corner, sipping ice water and crunching ice, and didn't think she saw him. Wanda had dressed well and had applied makeup, but even in the wan light Duke could tell she was beyond upset. It was audible in her music, which was more elegant than he expected. Wanda played the upright piano. An older dude with a gray ponytail handled guitar. A girl with tattoos running down an arm and a diamond stud through one nostril played curiously light and lilting flute when needed.

Wanda serenaded a decent crowd of a few dozen diners and listeners with haunting renditions of "Those Were the Days" and Chicago's "Wishing You Were Here" before showing she had a hell of a set of pipes with an old ballad by the Little River Band, "Reminiscing." The sadness in her voice was real and moving; Duke glanced to his right to see a woman at the next table weeping openly. Another sniffle sounded at his left. He doubted it was because of allergies.

Then she launched into "This Masquerade" and Duke forgot all about the pain in his empty stomach.

Without warning, the tears were spilling down his cheeks, and a sensory rush unlike anything he'd ever experienced before engulfed him. He thought of Jack Dalton, of growing up so privileged but never fully appreciating the chances that being born into rock royalty had afforded. A life where men like Seamus Whyler would have sold their souls for a fraction of what had been handed to him. Why the hell had he cursed his own successes? 3-D was a solid group, with an excellent catalog, only he couldn't remember a time when he'd appreciated any of it.

Look at where you are, right now at this second, chastised the critical voice in his thoughts. He had walked away from his life so easily, turned it over to a stranger in exchange for the stranger's identity. And a fine job he'd done in charge of this different life. Penniless, he was lurking in the shadows of a small town he probably wouldn't ever visit again after breaking an innocent heart already shattered.

The music. Oh, how Duke loved the music. Loved it with not quite all of his heart, because the rest of his heart loved Toby Cosgrove. Tears fell, and Duke's next breath hitched with a sob. He'd been a young boy the last time he'd cried.

Wanda sang about being lost in the masquerade, but Duke had lived it. She repeated the refrain, and Duke rose from his seat, wiped his eyes.

It was time to go, time to take back his life. Time to end this masquerade.

He dialed the number. Toby didn't answer.

"Hey, babe, it's Duke," he said after the voicemail beeped. "I'm on my way home. Fuck, I wish you'd pick up. Why aren't you picking up, man?"

Duke stabbed the phone's off button and gripped the wheel. Rain lashed the windshield, the storm making it nearly impossible to see the road beyond the few yards illuminated by headlights. The rest of the drive to Bay Breeze was a white-knuckled and emotional nightmare. Somehow, he made it.

While passing familiar landmarks along the boardwalk, Duke hoped he wasn't too late.

A sense of foreboding took hold of him on the march to the front door. Duke's senses were on heightened alert, which made ignoring the warning impossible. Lights were on inside, but they didn't offer much in the way or reassurance. His heart raced.

Duke entered the cottage. Toby sat on the sofa, his bare feet kicked up. He hadn't shaved, and his eyes remained locked on the television, even after Duke walked into the room, a clear sign that his worry was justified.

"Hey," Duke said. His stomach answered with a loud, painful groan.

Toby's eyes wandered up and met his at the periphery with a darting glance. "Duke," he said in a formal tone.

"So what's up?"

Toby shrugged.

"I tried calling."

"I know."

Duke sighed. "So, where have you been?"

This brought them fully eye-to-eye. "Where have I been? Dude, you take off for sights and cities unknown, and you want to know where I've been? Right here, man. I have a job, a life. Bay Breeze, that's where."

Toby turned away. Duke stepped closer. "Please, don't be like this, not after—"

"I think it's probably best that you go, okay?" Toby said, rising from the sofa. "I mean, it's been great and all, really great—"

"Toby, don't."

"But the truth is, I don't know who you are. How can I, when *you* don't? You're not Seamus, you're not—"

"I'm Duke. Duke Dalton. And I came back to tell you how much I love you. Totally, completely, dude."

Toby froze where he stood. Their eyes met and gazes locked. "You—?"

Duke stepped closer. "I love you. I'm so fucking crazy in love with you, with my music, with my life. I just needed a good swift kick in the ass, and I got it. And now that I've taken that size-twelve cleat between the cheeks, I can't believe that you don't want to be with me. I won't accept it."

"But what about your big life out there, and my tiny life here? It doesn't add up. It won't work."

"Says who?" Duke bridged the last of the distance. When Toby was close enough, Duke placed both hands on his shoulders and drew him close. Toby's tenseness melted. "There's nobody else, and there won't be. If you'll have me, I'm yours, now and forever."

Duke sank to one knee on the floor in front of him. Toby's frown morphed into a smile.

"Cut the shit and get back up here, you fool."

"A fool who's madly in love with you," Duke said.

He stood, and Toby admitted how much in love he was, too. "Okay, we can give it a shot."

"Good," Duke said. "*Great*—the greatest fucking bit of news I've ever received."

Their lips met, and though his empty stomach again complained, a different kind of hunger Duke had suffered for far too long was finally fed.

He scooped Toby into his arms and carried him into the bedroom. "I have to warn you, I've been on these big feet all day."

Toby licked Duke's throat. "Sounds like you need some toe sucking."

"Keep talking like that and I might have to suck on those sexy feet of yours, too, dude."

Toby smiled. "Okay, so I'll keep talking."

Track 18

THE BIG HAIR was long gone, replaced by a gray flattop, receding deep beyond the man's forehead. Even so, Seamus recognized Jack Dalton instantly.

"Dad," he said, unsure why, though any other greeting seemed inappropriate.

Jack Dalton eyed him warily. "*Dad*? That's a new one. Or an old one. Haven't heard you call me that in a long time."

Seamus stood and extended his hand. "Maybe too long."

Jack's gaze drifted to the invitation of a shake, just as distrusting. Still, he accepted. The two men sat as a waitress sidled over, platinum blonde and waxed eyebrows, a real LA girl. She asked if they were ready to order.

"Give us a minute, hon," Jack said.

The waitress said, "Sure," and flashed a coy smile at Seamus.

When they were again alone, Jack added, "You think she recognizes you?"

Seamus shrugged. "Hard to tell. With all that stage makeup...."

"That, and the rest of it. You know, that new trick of yours, since that concert in Austin."

Seamus reached for his water glass and crunched down on a cube. "You heard about that?"

"I'm old, not dead. Of course I heard of it. Eskimos and tribes of pygmies in the Amazon have heard about it. Hate to break this to you, but you're news."

Seamus sipped. "And let me guess—you disapprove mightily."

"Are you kidding?" Jack said, waving a hand in dismissal. "Wish I'd had the balls to lift my kilt on stage. Of course, in our time, it wasn't kilts but leopard print and Lycra, but I think Stage Fright would have gone a hell of a lot further if we had. Granted, it was a different time. I don't think we'd have gotten the same applause, just run out of town with pitchforks and torches."

"You guys were great, dad," Seamus said.

"There's that word again."

"Anyway... you know, Stage Fright was and is a hell of a band, and just because you guys didn't baste your turkeys for the Eskimos and Pygmies, you made Rock & Roll that's gonna last forever."

"Thanks to the Modern Wonder of YourTube."

"No, thanks to the fact you made great music."

"Maybe, sometime you and I will get to make music together."

"Maybe."

"Look, kiddo, I appreciate you returning the call, and I sure never expected us to be sitting here like this."

Seamus called the waitress over. She poured more water into his glass and asked if they wanted something stronger. Seamus ordered a round of sodas with lemon wedges and a plate of nachos—an appetizer they could both work on while working out the awkward dialogue of their reunion.

"You've changed," Jack said after the sodas arrived.

"I'm trying to."

"No, I mean it. There's an edge to you that wasn't there before. I always worried that you'd get soft. Not physically, but inside, underneath."

Seamus drew in a deep breath and just as deeply exhaled it. "Dad, *Jack*... which do you prefer?"

Jack shrugged, indicating either worked, though Seamus sensed "Dad" carried more weight, so that's what he used.

"Whatever shit went down, it's in the past. I can either keep getting pissed off over things—"

"Like the time you claim I almost starved you to death?"

"Whatever. My point is, I'd like to stop rehashing things and blow all that stink out to sea, once and for all. I'm ready to move forward. I forgive you."

"And I forgive you."

"Me?"

"It works both ways."

Seamus absorbed this latest wrinkle. "So, we're *jack* then, no pun intended?"

"If you mean "Jake," yeah, no more putting up the dukes, pun intended."

Seamus smiled. "Then let me say this—and I mean it truly from the heart—that it is a fuck-tastic honor to be in the company of the legendary lead singer of Stage Fright."

"And also, Duke De Morte, the main man—and I hear, the main *vein*—of 3-D."

They extended hands over the table and shook again, this time without hesitation.

"So why the change?"

"I met a dude whose dad used to knock him around a hell of a lot worse than you ever did."

"Thanks, I think."

"The important part is that this dude, his dad was a real prick. Never did anything for him except thicken his hide. Which sounds like a decent enough thing, until you understand how the thick skin came about. Through bruises that he inflicted. Anyway, this dude's a musician, so that outer layer of scar tissue helped prepare him for the artist's life. This guy had nothing. But at a young age, he created something. Made his first guitar with a piece of wood and some fishing line. In some ways, he had everything, so I guess what I'm trying to say is, I've put a fresh perspective on things recently. He had nothing, got nothing, had to make something. Me, I had almost everything, and you handed it to me. If I never thanked you, I'd like to say it now."

"I'd have given you a hundred times what I did, and more. You were my son. *Are* my son. I'm sorry I fucked up so many times."

"Ancient history," said Seamus. "And you've been sober, man, and that counts for something."

Jack rose from his seat. He waved for Seamus to do the same. The two men embraced.

"I love you, Duke."

Seamus clapped Jack's back. "Yeah, dad, same here."

Glancing over the other man's shoulder and across the restaurant at the table for one along a hedge of palm fronds, Seamus spotted Joe-Kev, who'd volunteered without condition to accompany him to the meeting with Duke's father.

Then Seamus saw another watching them and, more troublesome, the man's camera. Seamus identified the dude's dirty-blond spikes and doughy face immediately. It was Marquise Stilton.

Seamus broke the bear hug with Jack Dalton. "Hey, you," he bellowed.

Stilton jumped up and hurried toward the exit. Even before Jack asked what was wrong, Joe-Kev was up and after the moving target.

"I gotta go, dad," Seamus said, tossing a fifty onto the table. "But I'll be in touch, I swear."

"Let me help, son."

"You already have."

"Then tell me what's going on."

"Trouble," Seamus said on his way to join Joe-Kev. "The kind that's gonna bite me on the ass if I don't put a stop to it."

They chased the miserable fuck into the parking lot, only to lose him.

A few hours later, Stilton's latest blog entry went live, with six photos of Seamus and Jack Dalton talking, shaking hands, hugging. The headline read: "Even Duke's Dad Unaware He's Being Duped by 3-D Doppelganger!"

JOE-KEV WALKED INTO the master suite, chewing on a giant summer nectarine. The scent that carried into the room with him was a mix of sweet and masculine, and Seamus didn't attempt to hide his deep swoops of breath.

"Want a bite?" Joe-Kev asked, offering the fruit.

"I'm in the mood for a banana," Seamus chuckled.

"Mine?"

Seamus smirked and then kissed Joe-Kev deeply, loving the sweetness on his lips, before lowering to his knees in front of the other man. Always before in similar situations, Seamus was the dude who got his dick sucked. Only there really hadn't been similar encounters, he thought while unzipping; Joe-Kev Hallet was, without compare, one of a kind.

He worked Joe-Kev's fly open. The heady male scent of the other man's crotch greeted his next deep breath. Joe-Kev continued to munch on the nectarine while Seamus freed his hardening cock and low-swinging balls, the slurps seeming to telegraph what he planned to do to Seamus's ass. Joe-Kev loved to eat him, and Seamus was a dude who'd grown to crave having his asshole licked. Win-win, they were a pair of square pegs without worry of round holes, he thought with a chuckle. They were, quite simply, the perfect match.

Seamus sucked both of Joe-Kev's balls, one at a time, before taking a lick at the warm patch of flesh directly behind his sac. Joe-Kev obliged by stepping out of his pants and assuming a sexy Captain Morgan pose. Seamus licked his way up Joe-Kev's hairy inner thigh until his face was between the spread cheeks. Seamus brushed his tongue around Joe-Kev's knot.

His mouth full of nectarine, Joe-Kev mumbled a breathless, "*Fuck.*"

Since their first night together, Seamus had pulled a nifty trick that, at this early stage in their "man-romance"—Joe-Kev's term for it—never failed to drive the dude half-mad with lust. Seamus ate around Joe-Kev's ass, teasing the edge of his hole but not going for its bull's-eye. Joe-Kev's legs trembled. His balls flexed under their own power, and his cock, Seamus discovered, had toughened to its hardest. He teased the dude, tortured him, and right when he knew Joe-Kev couldn't take it another second, his tongue plunged in.

Joe-Kev howled. As had happened twice before, he started to squirt without needing Seamus's mouth or hand to bring him over the edge.

They lie together on the bed, both naked, cocks not entirely spent. Seamus reckoned that there was a very good chance of another session—unless some new calamity got generated by the latest round of Marquis Stilton's 3-D blog posts.

"What you did for Duke's dad was good. Pure class," Joe-Kev said.

"Duke might not think so. He finds out when he comes back... shit, I just couldn't hold that grudge for him."

Joe-Kev stretched out, scratched his balls. As the stretch subsided, he wrapped an arm around Seamus's shoulder and hauled him closer. They kissed and nuzzled faces, stubbled cheek against stubbled cheek.

"If he comes back."

"*When*," Seamus said. "I'm ready for these six weeks to end. Touring with the band, playing with you... especially you, dude, has been great and all. But I'm ready to get back to my guitar and out from under Harley's iron fist and away from all the hostility."

"When you do, I want to see your scrapbook."

The comment caught Seamus off guard. Sure, he remembered talking about it on the bus after making love and once in the dressing room, backstage in San Diego. But to hear Joe-Kev speak of it now put his concern about what came after the deal was done to rest.

"My scrapbook?"

"Yeah, I want to see all those places you played at before you joined 3-D, that piece of old fishing line."

Joe-Kev leaned his big right foot closer and caressed Seamus's left. Electricity crackled up his leg. Oh, yes, another round of lovemaking looked promising.

"You keep playing footsies with me, dude...."

"And you'll do what?" Joe-Kev challenged.

"Maybe I'll lick the sweat from between your toes."

A cocky smirk spread across Joe-Kev's face. "I'm ticklish."

"Too bad."

Seamus started to lower, only to double back. He playfully grabbed the back of Joe-Kev's head and massaged his scalp with the tips of his fingers.

"I'd love to show you my scrapbook, and the fact that you asked is only one of the many reasons I'm so fucking crazy about you, pal."

Joe-Kev blushed. "Shut up."

"No."

"Shut up… and suck my toes."

Seamus smacked Joe-Kev's outer thigh and crawled lower, to the bottom of the bed, where Joe-Kev's sexy feet waited for attention.

He wanted to go home. He wanted to perform his songs, and he didn't care if it was only to small audiences in clubs like the Casino or Cobalt Blues or Harry's Marathon, which was named after an amateur runner who'd won the big race in Boston decades earlier and opened a bar in his later years. Seamus loved playing that venue, even if the money was almost an insult. The place had great acoustics and even better pizza; the latter, all you could eat on any night you were booked to entertain the diners.

Joe-Kev tugged on his pants. "I gotta go."

"You could stay."

"I know, but I don't want you getting fucked with by that boy-bitch who lives downstairs. He catches me up here, he'll make some new rule that will land you in hot water, make it so that you can only bust a nut when you're onstage."

"Dude," Seamus sighed. "He can't control my love life."

Joe-Kev's lids narrowed. "You think so? He controlled Duke's. He made the calls on who got to go backstage, who got to come up these stairs. I've seen it with my own eyes."

"Is Harley in love with Duke?"

Joe-Kev huffed out a sarcastic puff of air. "I think Harley's in love with Harley. As Duke's right-hand man and the band's brains, it's like he's become this puppet master who makes up Duke's mind for him—who to talk to in the media, what endorsements to take, who to fuck. It's sort of sick."

"I agree, dude. But I'm not Duke. You want to stay, stay. You know how much I'd dig that."

"I would, too," Joe-Kev said. He smacked a kiss on Seamus's lips. "But I do want to get some rest before we play Lauderdale. I stay here with you... not so much sleep."

"I get it."

"After Lauderdale, however."

The two men kissed, said their farewells, and knew without having to voice it that they'd make good on that post-Fort Lauderdale rendezvous.

"Later," Joe-Kev said, smacking Seamus's butt on the way out of the room.

Simple as that, and wonderful beyond belief.

Harley sat beside Shaye in the kitchen. Seamus could tell by their expressions that they'd been waiting for him.

"Is this some kind of ambush?" he asked on the saunter to the fridge.

"What were you doing with Jack Dalton?" Harley demanded in that galling officious tone.

"What do you think? I was mending fences with the poor guy. Putting wrong to right."

"That wasn't your call," snapped Shaye. "Duke's gonna go off like a tactical nuke when he finds out."

Seamus pulled out a bottle of water. Unscrewing the cap, he said, "Since when do you care about Duke's welfare?"

"Since you showed up and started your Yoko Ono act."

Seamus sucked down a hit of water. "News for you, pal. I'm not the one who's going to break up this band. As a wise man told me, I'm one of the reasons you're all still eating caviar, so go fuck yourself. Not that it's anybody's business, but Jack Dalton called me."

"He called *Duke*," Harley corrected.

"And that would be me."

"Not much longer," Harley said. "I just heard from Duke. He's ready to come home. After the Lauderdale and D.C. shows, you're out. He takes over in Boston."

Seamus absorbed the news with a reaction that mixed happiness and a sense of remorse. For days, all he'd been able to think about was the end of the tour. Now that it was here, the reality challenged his resolve.

"Fine, whatever you want. But just so we're clear..." He fixed Harley with a leer. "When 3-D does self-destruct, it won't be my fault. It'll be because of you."

Harley froze. Shaye lashed out and charged. The next few minutes passed in a blur.

Track 19

PATRICK KARSER EXTENDED his hand. Marquis Stilton accepted. To Patrick, it felt like shaking a limp lump of boiled spaghetti. Luckily, there wouldn't be time for more contact than was necessary.

"Hurry up," Patrick said.

The infamous celebrity blogger began to strip out of his clothes. Patrick did the same—black shoes first, white socks, and then the rest of the limo driver's uniform, in order. He left his tight-whites on, but that didn't stop Stilton from reaching up and groping his package.

"Whoa, dude," Patrick said. "On any other day, maybe. We just don't got the minutes to spare for that."

"Fine," Stilton snapped. He began to dress in the discarded clothes.

It was a lie, Patrick knew. While he appreciated a decent hummer from another man's lips, there was just something about Stilton that caused him serious shrinkage. He couldn't imagine squirting a pint of his baby-juice or even so much as getting it up for those lips. He did not, however, have an issue with taking the dude's dollar bills. Especially when they came stacked thickly in an envelope.

This score was even bigger and fatter than the last, and Patrick had earned it. Not that he cared about the chauffeur's job anymore. He planned to pack up, cash out, and go wherever the fuck he wanted to after tonight.

He hauled on Stilton's jeans but not his shirt. The crisp white T he'd worn under his button-down was more than adequate for this balmy summer night. Fuck the limo—the band could afford another thousand limousines if they happened to walk out and find this one stripped of its wheels and electronics. Patrick was done. Patrick was *gone.*

Handing over the holographic security pass on the black lanyard, he reminded Stilton that there was but one last detail: that final payout.

"There it is, all twenty-k if you want to count it."

"Yeah, right, like I got the time, dude. Guess I'll just have to trust you." Patrick stuffed the envelope into the front of his pants and winced as the cold cash brushed his hardening dick. "And you'll have to trust that if there ain't the full amount in there, I'll hunt you down in California and cash in by fucking you over big time—and not in the way you want me to."

Stilton buckled his borrowed pants. "Point taken."

"Fucking-A right it is. The dressing room's that way. Thanks a mill, man—or at least twenty thou."

And then Patrick turned and hurried toward the nearest exit. Out on the street, he hailed a taxi and told him to head toward the nearest bus stop.

"Wait," he said as they pulled up to a red light.

"Where to then, buddy?"

Patrick smiled and cupped his groin. There was still enough time to make a quick detour. "The Wilver Court Hotel."

The makeup covered the waning yellows and greens and even the lingering purples of the bruise Seamus had taken from Shaye's sucker punch to one eye. He resisted the urge to wince as Perry applied the last of it.

The other man's hand landed on Seamus's bare knee. "Last chance, amigo. It's not like you'll need to save it."

Perry's hand inched higher. Seamus put his in the way, and its much larger size blocked Perry's advance.

"Thanks, dude, but I'm good. Not that I don't appreciate the offer."

"Okay, then. But you'll always be the one that got away."

Seamus smirked, stood. It was easy to resist the temptation because, by the end of this night, he would be Seamus Whyler once more—and Seamus had someone waiting to provide hand jobs and hot times and other, more important affairs of the heart. On the way out of the dressing room, he caught sight of Joe-Kev, now in full Autopsy makeup, and he knew the decision to hold back from Perry's offer was a no-brainer.

"Dude," Joe-Kev said.

"Dude," Seamus answered in like. He clapped a hand on the other man's shoulder. "Let's do this."

Seamus moved over to Arif and performed a similar gesture and words.

"Thanks, man, for everything," Arif said.

And then Seamus laid his hands on Shaye's naked shoulders and squeezed. "Let's do it, dude."

Shaye aimed the same fist he'd used to create Seamus's shiner over his shoulder. The two men punched knuckles. The few decent swings they'd gotten in against one another at Dymond Encerito on that last day had been swift and violent, leaving both men sprawled across the kitchen floor, listening to Harley howl. The sheer ridiculousness of the melee put an end to the fight more than Harley's shrieks, though he later took credit for stopping the scrum, the little prick. In the fallout of the fight, Seamus and Shaye resolved their differences, because everything that needed saying had been said. They'd settled their problems like men.

Lauderdale and D.C. had been the best shows of the tour. For Seamus, flying into Boston punctuated the strange journey that had started so long ago in Bay Breeze at the Casino Club. Tonight was a time of endings, but also new beginnings.

Seamus followed the band onto the stage, loving the applause, worrying if he would ever hear it at that level again.

Duke's heart galloped. Over the past six weeks, he'd wondered if he'd ever return to the stage again. Now, he couldn't get out there fast enough.

"What about the dick, dude?" Perry asked.

Duke blinked himself out of the spell he'd fallen victim to. "Huh?"

Perry aimed a pointer at Duke's cock, which had stiffened under the pulsing beat of his heart and the joyous anticipation of returning to the music, returning to the life.

"Should I paint *it*, too?" Perry asked.

Duke gazed into the makeup mirror. Duke De Morte's ghostly face stared back. But so did Toby's over one shoulder, the holographic pass around his neck glittering in the makeup mirror's light.

"I... I don't know," Duke said. "Should I?"

"Aw, hell," Toby said. "Give them what they want. Go big man, or go home."

Home, thought Duke. For the first time ever, the stage felt like one. Smiling at Toby in the mirror, he told Perry to make it so.

Seamus took his bow, his last as Duke De Morte, and jogged off the stage, the echo of applause at his back, the uncertainty of tomorrow ahead of him. Tears stung at the corners of his eyes. They'd threatened to fall as "Total Eclipse of the Heart" crescendoed in a thunderous cannonade of cymbal and soul; they were spilling down his cheeks by the time he reached the dressing room.

A security guard opened the door. Seamus hurried in, only to come face to face with his reflection. The mirror was flawed. Seamus stood soaked in sweat, dressed in black and white tuxedo costume with pants, while his image was kilted out, fresher in appearance. Both versions had grown misty, and for similar reasons—for love of the music, for love of their lives, mostly just for love.

Seamus and Duke stood and faced one another. Both men tipped their chins in understanding.

"You gave me back my life," Duke said.

"You gave me a taste of life," said Seamus.

The two men moved closer and embraced. Then, in unison, each whispered, "Thank you," into his reflection's ear. Parting, they gave the ghost up and exchanged identities.

Duke, the new Duke, shot a smile at a familiar face, the events coordinator from the Casino Club, whose name Seamus had trouble recalling on the spot.

The new Seamus turned as the rest of the band members hurried in, Joe-Kev leading the charge. Two men stood at the heart of the room, mirror images, nearly identical. But Seamus knew that Joe-Kev only saw one of them, and he couldn't have felt happier or more hopeful about the days and years to come.

On the march toward the stage, Duke detected a flash of movement from the corner of his eye. He turned in time to see a man in a black and white getup maneuver through the shadows, partially hidden by a length of black curtain, some sort of electronic device in hand. The getup was a uniform—that of a chauffeur. Duke recognized the uniform and the backstage pass, but not the man wearing them.

"Who are you?"

The man snapped his photo with a camera phone. "Who am I? More to the point, who the fuck are *you*?" Marquise Stilton said.

"I'm Duke Dalton," Duke said, right as a trio of security guards hurried over. "The one and only!"

The guards surrounded Marquis Stilton, who didn't offer much in the way of a credible threat, and Duke marched out onto the stage to a deafening round of applause. This time, he would earn it. This night was for Toby, and for the muse, and for the melody.

More than anything, it was for himself.

Duke had the accountant cut two bank checks. He overnighted the first in the amount of a million dollars to Seamus, along with a recording contract. The deal, which would turn out being supremely sweet if Seamus showed half the talent and testicular fortitude in the studio as he had during his time with 3-D, required him to be back in Los Angeles within a week to sign and to start.

The second arrived later the next afternoon at the Dewey Decibel Diner in Winter Woods, New Hampshire. It was made out to Wanda Cofield, also for a million dollars. The memo on the check read, <u>I.O.U. to Wanda and Angus, with love</u>.

Duke entered the studio with a renewed sense of wonder and a wide grin on his face. As though seeing the music and the memorabilia for the first time, he moved slowly, staring at the landmarks, absorbing every detail, even the most minute of observations. This was his playground, not a barracks. A place where music could be made and also enjoyed in a way it hadn't been before.

Or been allowed to.

Among the custom instruments, Duke found a simple, second-hand acoustic guitar propped up on a stand. He picked it up and plucked at the strings, checking the tune. It was perfect, the second most beautiful sight of the new day after waking beside Toby, who was still asleep in his bed up in the main house.

Duke sat and strummed. He planned to introduce a few new songs to the band's catalog, songs written during his journey of self-discovery, most of them inspired by Toby.

"Thank Christ," said a voice from the door.

Duke glanced up. Harley strutted in.

"About time things got back to normal around here," Harley groused. "That dickhead Seamus—"

"Seamus Whyler is a hell of a man, and a hell of a musician."

"And a hell of a pain in my royal ass. You're lucky there's still a house and a studio to come back to. Hell, a *band*."

Duke plucked absently, avoiding eye contact. "From what I hear, Seamus held things together, and if it wasn't for him, you and I would be having an entirely different conversation."

Harley folded his arms. "Whatever, dude. I'm just glad he's gone and that we can go back to running things the way we always have."

Duke set the guitar back on its stand. "Yeah, about that. I think it's time we had a change of attitude around here, one that's healthier for the band in general."

Harley started to argue, but at that moment, Duke's cell phone blasted out a riff from the band's *Spinal Column* hit. A text message, incoming. Duke opened the phone. After six weeks of using Seamus's basic-function antique, it took him several tries to access the message.

Son, meeting with you was the happiest day of my life. Thanks for giving me another chance. One day at a time, right? Call me when you can—Dad.

"Dude, do you know what he did?" Harley continued.

Duke's eyebrows knitted together. "I can guess."

Anger surged through Duke's insides. But as quickly as it rose, the emotion shorted out. Harley ranted in the background, but Duke found it easy to turn the volume down completely, and though he willed his fingers to delete the message, they didn't obey. Instead, they dialed the old man's number.

"Hello?" Jack Dalton asked after picking up on the second ring.

Duke hesitated and then he said, "Hey, dad, it's me, Duke."

Stone-faced, Joe-Kev said, "I'm leaving 3-D. You got yourself a drummer."

"Really?" asked Seamus.

Joe-Kev's expression held for another few tense seconds before breaking in a dopy, sexy grin. "Hells no, dude. I'm not gonna have that butthole Harley blaming you for breaking up the band. But I am gonna drive cross country with you, make sure you get to LA on time, so you can cut into our record sales."

"Thanks," Seamus said. "There's no one I want with me more than you."

Seamus checked the last of his stuff. Duke had taken excellent care of his guitar and scrapbook. His few bags of clothes looked great next to Joe-Kev's backpack and duffel. Lastly, he checked his wallet. There was plenty of green in there, along with a few plastic rectangles of gold and black. Seamus had never owned credit cards before. He'd also never had much money in the bank. He pulled out the deposit slip and sucked in a deep hit of breath. The slip belonged in the scrapbook, concrete proof that he hadn't dreamed the whole thing. It was real.

Even better, so was the dude in the passenger's seat, sitting with Seamus's beloved scrapbook in his lap.

"Hurry the fuck up, would you?" Joe-Kev chuckled.

"I'm hurrying."

Seamus took his seat behind the wheel and buckled his belt. He turned the ignition, started to drive, but didn't get far down the road.

"Wait," Joe-Kev said.

Seamus pressed down on the brake.

"There's one last thing."

Seamus eyed Joe-Kev warily as he reached into his pocket.

"I want to make this official," said Joe-Kev.

Seamus choked down a swallow. "Official?"

"Yeah, I didn't know if you were a silver dude or if you prefer gold, so I got this for now."

Joe-Kev opened his hand. Sitting in his palm was a coil of blue fishing line, woven into a rudimentary ring.

"Dude," Seamus said. Joe-Kev rolled the ring onto Seamus's finger.

In lieu of words, he leaned over and kissed Joe-Kev, crushing their lips together.

As he pulled back onto the road, Seamus adjusted the rearview. Looking in the mirror, he saw his reflection and felt no shame, only happiness.

About the Author

Gregory L. Norris lives and writes in the outer limits of New Hampshire. His work appears in novels, national magazines, numerous fiction anthologies, the occasional TV episode, and so far one produced feature film. His life was forever changed on a balmy August night after watching the musical *Xanadu*, when he knew beyond a shadow of doubt he'd follow his dream of being a writer.

Facebook: www.facebook.com/gregory.norris.10

Website: www.gregorylnorris.blogspot.com

Other books by this author

The Love of a Woodsman (November 2018)
Half-Life (Coming 2019)
Hope, Tears, Steam, Gears (Coming 2019)

Coming Soon from Gregory L. Norris

The Love of a Woodsman

A 2018 Holiday Short

Right as he was about to succumb, Teddy caught a flash of light, the day's glow reflecting off metal. Before his wide, terrified eyes, the blade of an ax materialized. An instant later, the driver's window exploded. A hand reached in and grabbed hold of his collar. Teddy screamed out the last of the air in his lungs, convinced his would-be killers had returned to finish what they'd started before the frigid water could. But Teddy was too weak, and the man attached to that hand was strong, pulling Teddy against him and carrying them both up to the surface.

They broke the water. Teddy gasped for breath. It was cold and went down painfully, but it was air and his lungs welcomed it. He blinked rapidly in tune with his gasps for breath. Past the clicking shutters, he caught sight of the arm wrapped around his, a big hand whose back was covered in threads of dark hair, the skin a healthy, living pink, rough but without a single mottled blemish.

"Don't worry," a man's voice growled in his ear. "I've got you!"

Also Available from NineStar Press

Connect with NineStar Press

Website: NineStarPress.com

Facebook: NineStarPress

Facebook Reader Group: NineStarNiche

Twitter: @ninestarpress

Tumblr: NineStarPress

www.ingramcontent.com/pod-product-compliance
Lightning Source LLC
Chambersburg PA
CBHW060555190726
48283CB00003B/1022